WE THE PEOPLE
The Way We Were
1783–1793

Westminster Press Books
by
SUZANNE HILTON

We the People
The Way We Were 1783–1793

Getting There
Frontier Travel Without Power

Here Today and Gone Tomorrow
The Story of World's Fairs and Expositions

Who Do You Think You Are?
Digging for Your Family Roots

The Way It Was—1876

It's a Model World

It's Smart to Use a Dummy

How Do They Cope with It?

WE THE PEOPLE
The Way We Were
1783–1793

BY
SUZANNE HILTON

THE WESTMINSTER PRESS
Philadelphia

BOOK DESIGN BY DOROTHY ALDEN SMITH

First edition

Published by The Westminster Press®
Philadelphia, Pennsylvania

PRINTED IN THE UNITED STATES OF AMERICA
9 8 7 6 5 4 3 2 1

Library of Congress Cataloging in Publication Data

Hilton, Suzanne.
    We the people.

    Bibliography: p.
    Includes index.
    SUMMARY: Describes the manners, customs, and daily living conditions of the American people in the first decade of their independence.
    1. United States—Social life and customs—1783–1865—Juvenile literature. [1. United States—Social life and customs—1783–1865] I. Title.
E164.H63   973.4   81-11392
ISBN 0–664–32685–4   AACR2

CONTENTS

1

THE AMERICANIZING OF AMERICA

> The American War is over—but this is far from
> being the case with the American revolution.
> . . . On the contrary, nothing but the first act of
> the Great Drama is closed.
>> *Pittsburgh Gazette,*
>> August 26, 1786

Winter was beginning to make itself felt on the twenty-fifth of November in 1783. William Cunningham, the British provost marshal, took another look around him as he mounted his horse for his last ride down Broadway, New York City's widest street.

"You're welcome to the place," he muttered to himself.

The silent people who lined the street as he rode by did not look threatening. They were just thinking to themselves, "It's about time you British were leaving," and their faces showed what they thought.

The war had ended more than two years before, when Lord Cornwallis had surrendered at Yorktown. At first, Cunningham and most of the British could not realize that York-

town was really the end. The next winter, though, a treaty
of peace was signed in Paris. That was a year ago. Now,
seven months after that treaty had been read aloud to the
soldiers on both sides, the British army was finally leaving
New York City.

"Foolish people," Cunningham grumbled.

They had given him nothing but trouble all summer and
fall. Americans who owned homes in New York City
seemed to think they could come back and move in, shov-
ing out the British officers who had been quartered in their
houses. Some had tried hanging out the American flag and
had been arrested for their trouble. American ships had
even shown the American colors in the harbor, but their
captains had changed their minds when a British frigate
shot a cannonball near enough to singe their sailors' whisk-
ers.

The British were to surrender the fort at Bowling Green
at noon, as soon as Cunningham's troops reached the fort.
An American contingent (surprisingly well uniformed) had
already marched down the Old Post Road and was waiting
now at the Bowery. Cunningham was late, he knew, but
there was no hurry now. Let them wait. By midafternoon of
this day, he thought, the last of us will be aboard a British
frigate, perhaps sailing for home.

Suddenly he noticed an American flag flying in front of a
tavern on one of the side streets. Furious, he galloped over
and tried to pull the flag down. Mrs. Day, the tavern
keeper's wife, grabbed a broom and hit Cunningham over
the head. His wig askew and the air filled with white hair
powder, he tried to fight her. But his officers pulled her
away. They persuaded Cunningham to continue on to the
fort.

The No-Name Country

Before the last British ship had sailed out of the harbor, the American citizens realized they were enjoying their first national holiday. They would celebrate Evacuation Day for many years to come.

The British left behind them a country that had many British ways. Most of its people had relatives and loved ones back in England and in other countries of Europe.

The country the British were leaving had no name yet. Some people called it "The Confederation," "United America," or "The Commonwealth." Others referred to it as the united states—without using capital letters. For many more years, people would say "the united states *are*," not "the united states *is*."

The country had no capital city, no leader, no money of its own, no real borders, no navy. Its army was a group of ragged volunteers, unhappy because they wanted to go home and they had not been paid the money owed to them. Its laws were called the Articles of Confederation, but people already could see that these laws were not good enough to pull the new country out of the mess it was in. There was not even a bill showing the rights of citizens—one of the main reasons they had fought a war. No one even knew how many citizens were in the country, since they had never been counted!

The country had no national anthem or oath of allegiance. No laws that were not British laws. No holidays of its own. No linen or wool factories turned out material to clothe its people. No American-made nails, iron, or glass helped build their houses. Americans had not even decided how to arrange the stars and stripes on their national flag.

The colleges had closed. Libraries had been ransacked. Churches had been destroyed and their ministers had been left suddenly with no ties to mother churches in England or Europe. Only two cities had theaters. The largest public building in the country was the State House in Philadelphia, where the Declaration of Independence had been signed.

There was not a single school book that had not come from England. There were no names for the flowers and animals that lived only on the American continent. No American works of art, paintings, musical compositions, or literature existed. There were no American heroes, except George Washington, because there was not yet any written American history.

The people had been calling themselves "American patriots" and "British Americans" for over thirty years. They had called the land "our country," not "our British colony." Now that the British had left, the people who lived in the thirteen states discovered that their country was not "American" enough. But more than anything, they wanted the world to know that their country was more than just a wilderness filled with "savages" and poor people.

Strange Country

Back in the old country, people thought that living in the new world must be almost as strange as living on the moon. After their return to England, soldiers talked about the "savages" and strange "poisonous" trees in the swamps. They said they had waded through ponds filled with leeches.

European travelers had taken a quick look at the new continent and written exciting books filled with stories about "tiger cats" (mountain lions) that pounced on defenseless travelers lost in the deep forests.

"There are," said the books, "vicious houses of entertainment in the country. A traveler can identify them just by looking to see whether the tavern keeper has had his ears cut off." Cutting off an ear was a punishment used by the British for various crimes.

The Americans had many rumors to correct if the world was to respect their new nation. Many people believed that the American continent was still in such a savage state that animals grown there were not so large or so well developed as those in the old world.

In 1787, American newspapers were careful to mention that a Mr. Hiltsheimer had raised a steer that weighed 1,771 pounds. A Mr. Cooper owned a horse that was 17 hands, one inch tall—almost six feet.

"Your children will not grow tall in that country," said the people from the old world. The new Americans wondered if they could be right and so were very careful to measure their children often. A middle-sized man in England was 5 feet 5 inches in height. Anyone over 5 feet 8 inches was considered tall. If anything, Americans seemed to be growing even taller than their ancestors.

Queer Rumors

"Look at the natives in that country," the people in the old world argued. "You will turn the same color after a few generations." A professor told Americans that even if they were "thrown back into the savage state," they would never look exactly like Indians. Yet every settler knew that women and children who had been kidnapped by the Indians did not look the same as they had before they were captured. Parents in the new world did not even allow their children's faces to get a suntan if they could help it. Little girls were sewn into their bonnets in the morning and some were even dressed for outdoor play with face masks of linen.

"The more refined plants—like flowers and fruit—will not grow in that soil," said the old people. "It has been wild since the beginning of time." Every American garden held fruit trees and flowers, even though the wintry winds killed some. Botanists covered the country looking for trees and plants that were native to the new world. In Kentucky alone they found black cherries, mulberries, a "coffee tree" that made good coffee, honey locust which made beer, plenty of food for cattle, and beautiful wild flowers.

"America has an improperly balanced climate" was another argument that old world people used when they met emigrants who intended to leave for the new world. "You will sicken and die." The British, especially, were used to cool summers and mild winters on their islands. They could not imagine living where the temperature could go from zero degrees to 100 degrees during the year. Such weather must surely take away a person's vigor and encourage diseases.

The rumors were silly. But life was very different in the united states. Its citizens decided it was high time for them to wake up, study themselves, and adopt some new manners that fit into their own way of living.

That is the "revolution" this book is about. In its pages you will meet the Americans who lived in those days. They are going about their everyday lives, coping with ordinary happenings and some not so ordinary. And they are trying hard to form a more perfect union.

2

HOME SWEET CABIN

A smoky house and a scolding wife
Are two of the greatest ills in life.
Quoted by Benjamin Franklin in 1788

"All the furniture I had was two pocket knives and a tin
cup," said Samuel Shepard.

Samuel was eighteen when he left New England to make
his fortune in Kentucky. Almost as soon as he arrived, he was
offered the job of schoolmaster. The usual arrangement for
schoolmasters was for them to "board around," so Samuel
lived with one family for a while and then another. All went
well until January. Then he discovered that the children of
the new family all expected to sleep with him to keep warm.
Samuel decided to build a house of his own, even though it
was midwinter. He borrowed a saw and set to work.

"All my bed and bedclothes was a surtout coat [a large
overcoat] and a few clothes which was all my property—
except an axe, a smooth bore [gun], and some books. But
what was worse than all," said Samuel, a hungry growing
boy, "I had not one mouthful of provision of any kind. Nor

to the amount of one cent in cash."

Samuel squared the trunks of some trees roughly with his ax and laid them carefully in an 8½-foot square. By January 10, the walls were as high as his head. The structure looked like a small fort, with no way in or out except over the top, until he cut out the door. He sawed along a plumb line, straight down to the ground, slicing slowly through the logs. Moving the plumb line a few feet to the side, he sliced down the other side of his doorway. By January 19, he had finished the walls, put on a shingled roof, and moved in.

Samuel had been careful not to cut the door out on the windiest side of the house, but it was mighty cold without any front door. Snow still covered the ground inside, but he would soon cover that with a floor. His neighbor gave him a turkey, a piece of bread, and a piece of pork. He borrowed some cornmeal and returned to his cabin to cook dinner.

"I set up some flat stones against one of the walls of my hut, against which I built a small fire," Samuel said happily. "My first object was to make a door, for which I had neither planks or nails. A neighbor gave me some board. Then I used pins [made of wood] instead of nails. By January 21, I got my cabin tight and warm," he reported, after filling the cracks between the logs with clay.

Samuel lined his wooden chimney with clay, also. He planned to make a safer chimney with stones someday. But for now, he had to be very careful not to set the chimney on fire. His neighbor told him that a chimney built on the south wall of a house would draw better and that the opening at the arch of the chimney should be smaller than any place above the arch. That way it would never smoke up the house the way a pyramid-shaped chimney would.

Samuel Shepard felt like a wealthy man. He had seen one

family, along the Monongahela River, that lived in a hollow sycamore tree. An opening on one side of the tree formed the door, and they had built their fire just outside the door.

"The hollow was so large," said Samuel, "that it contained two beds, a chest, and some other furniture besides several persons."

Discomforts of Home

Dwellings in frontier country were rarely more than one-story log houses, even though their owners had come from towns and comfortable homes back along the Atlantic Coast. Once a traveler asked some pioneers how they could stand living in tiny log cabins after being used to homes built of brick and filled with the luxuries of modern living, like rugs and china.

"We stand it," answered one, "because we know that in the turn round of a very short time, we shall be living in comfort again out here."

Most frontier people lived just like Samuel at first. For dishes they used wooden trenchers that looked like small meat platters. They ate with their pocketknives when they did not have forks. When they needed a container, they smoothed out the inside of a piece of hollow tree. Later they grew gourds and shaped them into bowls, cream skimmers, dippers, and even bottles. Most people did not own more than one chest. They hung their clothes on wooden pegs on the wall.

With the first money that Samuel earned, he bought a copper teakettle—one item that nature could not provide for him. His second purchase was more a matter of pride.

His brother was coming to visit him from Connecticut and Samuel walked into the city to buy three white earthenware plates. Households in the united states had very few luxuries like china and silver. Ordinary homes had earthenware, or, at best, stoneware dishes. Sometimes dinner was served in one large bowl, the family "eating in the Dutch fashion," with each person using a long-handled pewter or wooden spoon to reach the food.

Back in the east, homes had many more comforts.

American houses were built on the order of houses in the old world, but had been adapted to fit into the new world. Connecticut houses were usually of wood, two stories high, with two rooms across the front and the chimney in the

While Hampton was being built in 1787, workers were allowed to stop work at 3 P.M. to avoid meeting wolves in the forest on their way home

middle. Philadelphians usually built their houses of brick, three stories high and with the kitchen in the cellar. West of the Allegheny Mountains, most houses were of squared logs. People there said they would probably never be able to make bricks on the Pittsburgh side of the mountains. Virginia houses often had porches all the way around. Farther south, the kitchen was usually a small separate house behind the main house.

Each home had a kitchen garden, where the family's herbs, spices, and medicines grew. Although flower gardens were considered a luxury, many families planted fruit trees, flowers, and snowball bushes. The little "blue bottle" flower from England was renamed "ragged lady," "corn pink," or "bachelor button" over here.

"We were cooped up in a close, bandboxical room," complained one lady who was not used to the small rooms in American homes. She soon learned that the small rooms were easier to heat in winter. In summer, the thick walls kept them cool. Many homes had two parlors. The front one was often saved for funerals and weddings, while the back parlor was for family and "tea" company. Most rooms were freezing cold in the winter, but the parlors and the kitchen were "fire rooms."

Hot and Cold

"Fire rooms," those with stoves, were heated by an old Prussian stove or the new American Franklin stove of cast iron. The stove stood far enough out in the room so that six or eight people could get around it at one time, its smokestack emptying into the chimney. The stoves burned wood for heat. No one used coal yet, in the united states, although there were rumors that some of the hills of Pennsylvania had coal as good as that found in Wales. Slow-burning logs were put in the back of the stove, and chestnut or black spruce logs up front. Hickory logs burned the longest, but they made loud, crackling noises, shooting out burning splinters of wood. Since everyone put carpet around stoves "to concentrate the heat," it is no wonder the fire departments were busy all winter.

Screens were set in front of the fireplaces to catch the shooting sparks. There were no matches to light fires. Instead, people used flint, steel, and tinder. Tinder was any vegetable matter that would catch fire easily—like a very dry leaf, a piece of scorched linen, or old cambric handkerchiefs. The tinder was kept in a small round tinderbox with the flint and steel. When flint and steel were struck together sharply, they made a spark that landed on the tinder. Then, with gentle blowing, a fire slowly gathered strength. Sometimes it took a half hour to get enough fire to light a candle. Most families kept a small fire alive in the kitchen fireplace so they could light a taper from it to carry around to light candles and other fires.

Firelight was not bright enough for reading or writing letters. People lighted the main room "at candlelight" each night with tallow or dipped candles in an assortment of candle holders. Candle arms on the wall held a pair or more of candles. Mirrors fastened behind the candles reflected the light and helped to brighten a room. Overhead, a metal or wooden hoop, called a candlebeam, held several candles at once.

One candle alone burned evenly. But as soon as several were put in a candlebeam together, the heat caused them

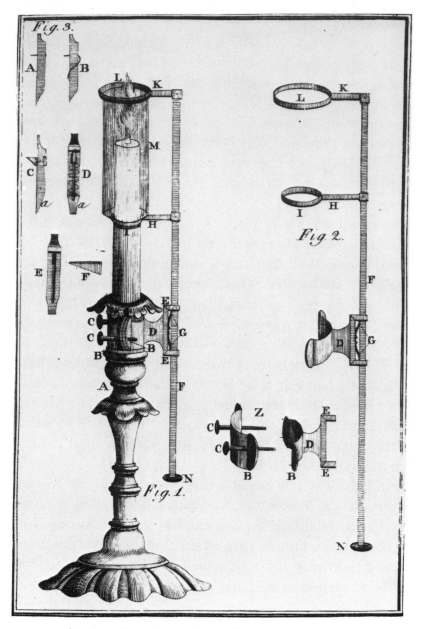

An ingenious invention to keep a candle from flickering was to attach a glass tube over the end of the candlestick

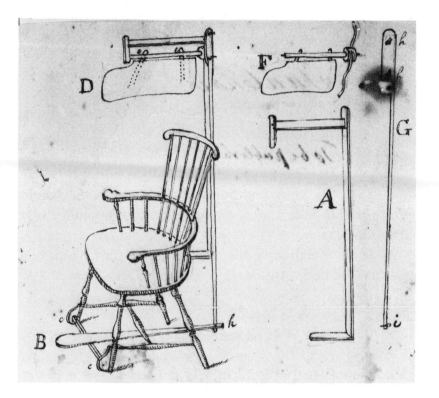

An air-conditioned Windsor chair—when the occupant's foot touched the board (B), the fan (D) made a breeze

to melt down faster. Rich people could use spermaceti candles which gave out three times the light of tallow candles and flame four times as great. But a pound of tallow candles cost just over a shilling (about 18 cents), while a pound of spermaceti candles cost over 35 shillings ($6).

Light was the main reason people went to bed early. When a person tried to read by candlelight, the flame was agitated constantly by the air in the room. In the winter, the flame was always being drawn by a current of air toward the chimney's draft. Sometimes the candle's light had a fast vibrating motion. The letters on the book or paper then appeared and disappeared in quick succession. The reader did not know whether his eyesight was failing or not.

Fashionable city people no longer whitewashed their halls, staircase, and parlor walls. They used "paper hangings," later called wallpaper, that were pasted to the walls. To add a touch of elegance, they pasted paper borders and festoons around the ceiling. Some people even painted their rooms in color. One man complained that his neighbor was putting on airs.

"Well, our neighbor Jones has set us a fine example of expense," he said. "He has laid one of his rooms in oil."

Fire Screens and Feather Beds

Most people had little furniture, but the Windsor chairs made in America were especially popular. Windsors came in several styles. One was a low-backed armchair with one wide arm that could be used for writing letters. Under the writing arm and also under the seat were small storage drawers. Usually a parlor also had a chair and "sopha" that were stuffed with horsehair for comfort, a writing desk, and small tables. Dining tables came in pairs. When only one was used, the other stood against the wall. Card tables were common in southern homes, but there were very few in New England, where playing cards was still considered an invention of the devil.

Before the open fireplace was often a small fire screen, about the size of a person's head. It was placed beside the person sitting nearest to the fire to keep the heat off the face —but not only for comfort. So many people had smallpox scars that they used a little wax to make their faces look smooth. The heat from the fireplace melted the wax quickly and exposed the ugly scars.

In the old world, beds had hangings over the top and down the sides. These kept sleeping people warm in winter and gave privacy when the rest of the family slept in the same room. But in America, houses were kept warmer, and gradually people stopped using the curtains on their beds. In the south, the covered bedsteads were called "pavilions"

The ironmaster at Hopewell Village had many luxuries in his home

and were hung in the summer with curtains of netting to keep "the mosketoes" away.

Beds had sacking bottoms with huge feather mattresses on top. Fifty or sixty pounds of feathers made a mattress. Poorer people had mattress covers stuffed with straw which had to be renewed every so often. Children also slept on straw mattresses laid on the floor at night. Every morning, mother or a servant picked up the children's beds, shook them, and laid them, one on top of the other, on the main bed for the day. She fluffed up the other feather beds and laid them over the top. Then, over this mountain of bedding, she threw a quilt about twelve feet square to keep everything clean.

Only wealthy people had counterpanes or bedspreads—they were for show, not warmth. Most people used quilts made of about three layers of material with wool as the middle layer. Quilt designs were very simple—a Star of Bethlehem or just a Rising Sun in the center. Every young girl was expected to make at least one quilt before she could go to housekeeping. She and her friends got together for quilting parties and helped each other make their bedding.

Housekeeping Headaches

Homes everywhere had no indoor bathrooms. Instead, a small house, called "the necessary," was built in the backyard. It was just large enough for a person to walk into and then sit down on a board that had a hole cut out. In all but the very worst weather, when a person could use a chamber pot indoors, the necessary was the only place to go. Underneath the necessary was a large, deep pit. The small building was not always very sturdy and its supports, sunk down in the ground and close to the foul-smelling pit, were rarely inspected.

One day, the wife of a baker in Philadelphia stepped into the necessary. The floor collapsed, plunging her down into the pit. She sank up to her shoulders. Only the flooring, still beneath her feet, kept her from sinking still further. Choked by the stinking smell, she screamed as well as she could to attract attention, but it was almost an hour before she was found—closer to dead than alive.

The necessary was the ideal nursery for flies, which often went straight from there to the dining room table. People did not worry about what the flies might bring indoors. No one had ever heard of germs. People were annoyed only because "flies had dirty feet." One doctor said you need only look at the bellpull to see what dirty feet they had. The bellpull operated a rope attached to a bell in the kitchen to call the servants. Bellpulls were sticky from the flies that walked on them, said the doctor. It did not occur to anyone that the flies were drawn to the bellpull in the first place because human hands had already made it sticky.

It is hard to realize how many flies people had to cope with two hundred years ago. Homes had no screens in the windows and the food smells attracted flies. Clothes were not washed often and had assorted spots from food. Flies clung to clothing, walked on people's faces, eyelids, and across their spectacles. When the flies were brushed off, they stuck to people's hands. There were no flyswatters or insect sprays.

In Georgia, housekeepers hung up bunches of "tarflower" and the flies stuck to the blossoms. Another plant, with spikes of white flowers, was a natural poison. Housewives bruised the plant's roots, steeped them in water all night, and put them on a platter with molasses. The flies then, according to the almanac, "swarmed in, tasted it, and died in incredible numbers." Since the mixture also killed crows, rats, and small animals, it was dangerous to use around little children.

No one collected garbage. It was dumped outdoors and eaten by the pigs and rats that ran loose. Rats often entered houses at night. One man complained that the rats woke his family every night by dragging his shoes across the floor and knocking over his wife's pewter plates. He found a solution in his almanac which told him to make a mixture of oatmeal, coarse sugar, and limestone. After the rats ate the mixture, they would be very thirsty and would drink water until they burst. "After which," said the almanac, "the rest of the rats will leave the place."

Another unwelcome houseguest was the bedbug. Bedbugs could not be avoided in taverns, but a man expected some relief from them in his own home. Everyone had a guaranteed cure. Some people put spicy sassafras wood in the drawers of chests or made their beds of sassafras wood. But the most popular prevention was to swab every inch of beds, curtains, laces, and nettings, with a mixture of camphor, turpentine, and lamp spirits. The terrible smell lasted only four or five days and nights. But the job had to be done in the daylight, and a person had to enter the room at night without a candle, because, for the first few weeks after it was done, the whole place could explode into flames.

One item not found in the home was a wastebasket. There was nothing to throw away. Leftover grease and wood ashes were turned into soap. Yarn and pieces of material stayed in the ragbag until the right use came along—possibly a rag rug. Broken stoneware dishes were pulverized into powder. Added to egg whites and quicklime, the powder made a fine glue to repair the next broken dish. The deep-blue paper that sugar came wrapped in was cut into small pieces and used to dye material. Dried pumpkin became sweetening when the high-priced sweetener was not available. The coarse thread a housewife had left over from spinning flax into linen was called "tow." She made work shirts, smocks for the children, trousers, sacks, and even rope out of it. Small pieces of heavy material left over after making a man's suit became a pair of shoes. Uneaten food went into the stewpot or was used to feed the animals. The horns of dead animals were soaked for weeks until they could be separated into thin sheets almost as transparent as glass. The thin glass-like pieces were used to make "hornbooks" or lanterns, called "lanthorns." The horn tips made buttons or handles for eating utensils.

There was even a use for fresh horse dung still hot from the animal. It was rushed inside while still warm and laid in a tub near the fire. Then the cook sprinkled mustard seeds over it and covered the seeds with more horse dung. Kept by a warm fire, the mustard seeds sprouted and grew into plants tall enough to be cut for a salad—in only two hours!

There was no stove for cooking. Housewives cooked in the chimney. The newest invention was a swinging crane of iron. Now the cook could swing out her stewpot, add seasonings, and stir and swing it back again—all without bending dangerously close to the flames. Around the fireplace, she had iron pots of all sizes and shapes. There were skewers of handwrought iron to cook meat and potatoes on, waffle irons, and long-handled "salamanders" that she heated and waved over the tops of cookies or pies to brown them slightly. She used basket spits to hold small pieces of meat so they wouldn't drop into the coals and small spits with drip pans to cook small birds. A cook who had no bake oven in the chimney used a "tin kitchen" that stood in front of the fire for baking or roasting by reflected heat.

Sometimes families had to eat a "patched dinner," what we call "hash," but many tempting goodies came from the kitchen. There was cheesecake, lemon pudding, Indian slap-jacks made of cornmeal. For parties, there was Independence Cake, frosted with sugar and covered with gold leaves, or a delicacy called Candied Violets made from real violets. People made their own butter, coloring it with carrot juice, and many kinds of cheese. They also turned out some meals that are no longer on most menus, like sheep's tongue pie, ragout of pig's ears and feet, and pig's "pettitoes," for which the cook cleaned off the hair and split the pig's feet down the middle. Some foods were new, even to Americans. Samuel Shepard discovered that he liked buffalo beef and "sower croud" (sauerkraut) out in Kentucky, while Nathan Webb smacked his lips in Boston over "a most excellent pie made of ten robins." The general rule for serving bird pies was not to cook the birds with the prettiest songs.

At first, the American colonists drank as much tea as the British. Then came the Boston Tea Party, and it was no longer patriotic to drink the British beverage. Americans began making coffee from several different plants and grew to like it better than tea. Now that the war was over, there was plenty of tea, but coffee had come to stay.

"Coffee is a slow poison," one doctor told his patient.

"Very slow, indeed," said the patient, "for I have drank it every day these eighty years."

Coffee was not really a poison, but the American kitchen

of those days did have many slow poisons. Green pickles turned a lovely green color because the housewife cooked them in special copper pans. As soon as she added the vinegar and the pickles cooled, the desired green color came. If it did not, she threw in a few copper halfpence. She never knew that the copper and the acid vinegar were a dangerous combination.

She measured salt on copper scales and baked lemon tarts in copper patty pans, too. The kitchen was full of rusty spoons that had been made of mixed metals. The common brown pottery ware had a lead glaze and was deadly when

Goodies from the kitchen included Candied Violets and ragout of pig's ears

combined with lemons, oranges, or other acids. Chinaware, made in China or Staffordshire, England, was safe to use, but only rich people could afford to buy it. Cooks often added leaves of common laurel to their custards and "small hemlock" (called "fool's parsley") to salads without knowing they were poisonous. Pewter had a good amount of lead in it, yet babies drank their milk and juice from pewter baby bottles and pewter cups. In cities, lead pipes carried water from ponds to the public wells.

Lead poisoning does not kill people quickly. Lead builds up in a person's body for a long time before blindness and paralysis show up. These were symptoms many people had in those days. But the chances were that the very cook who had caused the lead poisoning was also the "doctor" who treated it. For the treatment of blindness, she took a double handful of top celery leaves and a spoonful of salt. Pounding them together, she made a poultice. If her patient was blind in the right eye, she laid the poultice on the left wrist. She put on fresh poultices every day for five days. Then, while her patient was recuperating, she gave the patient a treat for dinner—"sick bed custard" baked over the coals in a pewter vessel.

No one could keep food fresh at home—especially in the summer. Lucky country people had a "spring house," a small house built into the ground, with a cold spring of water running through it. Even butter and milk kept well in a springhouse. But in cities there was usually no such handy cold spring. The housewife or a servant had to go to market every day. Although food could be bought every day, including Sunday mornings before church, the big market days were Tuesdays and Fridays.

Each city had its special marketplace, usually an open-arched brick building roofed over for protection from the weather. Breezes and dust circulated through the arches, keeping the building cool in summer and frigid in winter. Philadelphia's famous market was five blocks long, with several roofed-over stalls. Between each building was a cross street with traffic constantly going through.

Customers found many delicacies to take home. There were pies already baked, X-cakes (hot cross buns), dainty

Peale drew this scene of an accident in Lombard Street. The chimney sweeps are laughing at the girl who has dropped her pie

birds for breakfast. Storekeepers covered their vegetables and fruits with damp cloths to keep the flies off. On market day, meats were sawed in round and appetizing shapes. Fresh limes cost 50 cents for a hundred, a pound of chocolate about 22 cents, and ginseng tea to be used as a medicine cost about 25 cents a pound.

The careful housewife had learned from her mother how to pinch food. She selected pork that broke or felt soft and oily when she pinched it between her fingers. She pinched the mutton to see if the flesh would soon return to its former appearance, showing it was fresh. She carried a little, sharp-pointed knife and plunged it quickly into the ham, underneath the bone, drew it out and smelled it. A turkey was young if his spurs were short and his legs black and smooth. But if his eyes were sunk into his head, the housewife knew he was long dead. She did not buy lamb, because it was patriotic to let lambs grow up to supply wool.

A shopper could not always tell good butter by tasting it in the cask. Most shopkeepers put their best butter on the top. The careful shopper unhooped the barrel to the middle and jabbed her knife between the staves so that she could smell the butter in the center. To make sure she was buying fresh eggs, she put her tongue on the larger end. If it was warm, the egg was fresh. She selected cheese that had a smooth coat outside. Rough coats that were too dry on the top were often a sign that there were maggots inside the cheese.

She bought sugar in a loaf or a cone that weighed 9 or 10 pounds. Later she cut the sugar up into lumps of smaller size. One loaf or cone lasted a year if a family was careful and stretched it by using honey or molasses. A hundred pounds of muscovado sugar (unrefined) cost about $6, while a gallon of molasses cost 34 cents. Country families could supply almost all their own needs in the summer, but they had to buy salt, 50 cents a bushel, to salt their meat, since there was no way to keep it cool.

A spinning wheel cost a little over $1.50. A housewife who owned one could spin the flax grown on the family's land into fine linen thread and make all her own sheets, towels, "board cloths" (tablecloths), pillowcases, aprons, shifts, petticoats, short gowns, and bed hangings. If she had some cloth left, she could make a little money by selling it at the village store for 42 cents a yard. She sold it at a higher price if she whitened the linen first by souring it in buttermilk. But the money she earned belonged to her husband, not to her.

Homespun material lasted longer than any material that could be bought. Grain sacks and homespun flannel sheets lasted a hundred years. The spinning wheel was a fashionable piece of furniture and a symbol of patriotism. Linen and wool made at home helped to make the united states independent of Great Britain.

New Fashions

Americans prided themselves on making their own clothes, now that the war was over. Women swore off wearing imported silk, ribbons, laces, feathers, beaver hats, and gauzes. Dresses became plain and came down to the floor. Enormous headdresses and huge bonnets were no longer in fashion here. Making the change was not hard at all. The ladies discovered that their clothing had been dictated by the cool climate in England. The heavy, hot dresses that were comfortable over there were unbearable in 90 degree

The latest in fashions

weather here. American women also realized that the
dainty shoes with paper soles so popular among rich ladies
in England were useless in this land of few paved sidewalks
and no paved roads.

Hats were important. Women wore theirs everywhere,
except in church, where it was improper for a woman to

worship with her head covered. Men all bought the new "round hat" that never fit their heads right—because heads are oval, not round. Women wore something called "the long-quartered shoe" which was so uncomfortable they could hardly walk a step without pulling it up. Men's dress-up shoes had huge buckles that never seemed to be the right size and that hurt their feet. In bad weather, men wore boots with cork liners or "waterproofing" of linseed oil, mutton fat, beeswax, and resin.

There were no special clothes for the cold winters. People who had to go outdoors just put on several layers of wool. The men wore two or three pairs of trousers, and ladies put on two or three woolen frocks. For travel, men wore "sherryvallies," pantaloons of leather buttoned on the outside of each leg and worn over their trousers. A well-dressed gentleman always had his greatcoat which he could use for a blanket when he stopped for the night. When it was extremely cold, people wore heavy woolen stockings over their shoes or wrapped their feet in cloth that had been soaked in neat's-foot oil, just as the soldiers had done at Valley Forge.

In the summer, people wore linsey-woolsey dresses and shirts, made of flax and wool. Cotton was more comfortable in hot weather, but it was too expensive. Not much cotton was raised in the south because the process of picking and cleaning cotton was slow and costly. Soon the invention of the cotton gin would change all that. Cotton would become cheap and the price of slaves would go up.

As homes changed from cabins to houses, people changed too. Where once it would have been proper for American families to sit down at the table and suggest that someone "cut up the chicken" so they could eat, such manners were becoming unthinkable. Now a person had to be careful to choose the right term. "Break the goose," "thrust that chicken," "spoil that hen," or "pierce the plover, please" showed the world that Americans were civilized at home.

3

GROWING UP SMART

Our Tom is grown a sturdy boy
His progress fills my heart with joy.
His master says—I'm sure he's right—
There's not a lad in town so bright.
From *The Rare Adventures*
of Tom Brainless, 1787

"Little Henry fell into the river," Elizabeth Drinker wrote in her diary. "He was in his wet clothes a quarter hour and came home very cold and coughing. We stripped him and after rubbing him well with a coarse towel, put on warm, dry clothes, gave him some rum and water to drink, and then made him jump a rope until he sweated."

Little Henry Drinker's swim on the thirtieth of August evidently did him no harm, because the very next day he was out teasing the neighbor's dog.

"Carlisle's dog, Lion, bit Henry's eyelid and eyebrow till it bled," said Mrs. Drinker the next day. "It was swelled and sore for a day or two, then got better."

A few days later, Elizabeth's daughter Molly fell off the

fence and cut her chin. After mother dressed the hurt with balsam apple, the doctor came and bled Molly. Baby Charles caught the measles, and instead of the spots showing on the outside, "they struck in" and for a whole week mother and the servants took turns holding the crying baby, day and night. Meanwhile, son Billy came home with his face bruised from boxing with one of the Latin School boys and daughter Sally had "the fall fever." Mrs. Drinker did not have time to take her clothes off for two weeks, except to change them. Then little Henry fell out of the cherry tree when the limb broke and he fractured his collarbone. At least, with Henry immobile for a while, Mrs. Drinker might have had a little rest.

Freedom's Babies

Every wife expected to have a large family. That was what women were for, girls had been told all their lives. One third of the babies died before they were three years old. No one knew why. At least part of the reason could have been the baby bottles. Some were of tin with a hand-carved wooden nipple. Some were made of pewter. Either of them could have given a baby lead poisoning. Even the babies that were nursed did not always get the right nourishment. No one realized that a mother's milk was not nourishing if the mother did not eat right. In the south, the wet nurse was often a slave who, although she was nursing, had no better food than the other slaves.

"Babies spend the first few months of their lives in a kind of torpid amazement," said a scientific baby book from England. After that, the book said, young children remem-

"Spit not in the room, but in the corner," said
the rules for polite behavior

bered best those lessons learned with pain. Most Americans
did not agree with the book. They wanted their children to
have more love and freedom while they were still small.
Later would be time enough to teach them discipline.

American babies were no longer dressed in tight clothing.
They often went without shoes and stockings, but never
without a small cap on the head. When a child began to
walk, the mother made a band of stuffed velvet to protect
the child's head from bumps and attached strings to the
baby's belt to help hold the child upright for the first steps.
The babies who were lucky enough to survive infancy had
an easy life until they were almost old enough to go to
school.

Then they were introduced to a new book called *The*

School of Good Manners, written by a Boston schoolmaster. The book had 163 rules to obey, and 8 "sins" to be avoided at all costs. Among the sins were disobeying parents, singing naughty songs, playing on the Lord's Day, and saying "Oh Lord!" When children were naughty, their father told them they had broken God's laws. He made them say they were sorry and promise never to do the same naughty thing again. The next time, father used a birch rod, telling his children that he did it only because God had told him "not to withhold correction." Laying all the blame on God probably did not give much comfort to the child, who could not sit down for some days afterward.

The 163 rules for good behavior covered every waking moment of a child's week. "In church," said the rules, "shift not seats, but continue in the place where thy superiors order thee. Do not talk in meeting house. Fix thine eye on the minister. Do not let it wander. Walk decently and soberly home, without haste or wantonness, thinking about what thou hast been hearing.

"At table, do not take anything for thyself, even though it be that which thou dost greatly desire. Do not ask for anything. Wait until it is offered to thee. Turn not thy meat the other side upwards to view it upon the plate. Bite not thy bread, but break it, but not with slovenly fingers. Do not look at another person's plate or upon the meat. Do not look earnestly on anyone that is eating. Spit not in the room, but in the corner, or rather, go out and do it abroad.

"At school, bow when thou comest in. Pull off thy hat, especially if thy master be in school," continued the rules. "If the master speaks to thee, rise up and bow, making thine answer standing. Bawl not aloud in making complaints. A boy's tongue must never be heard in school but in answering a question or saying his lesson. Go not rudely home through the streets, stand not talking with boys to delay thee, but go quietly home.

"Outdoors, do not go singing, whistling or hollowing down the street. If thou goest with parents, master or any superior, do not go evenly with them, but a little behind them. Run not hastily in streets or go too slowly. Wag not to and fro nor use any antic postures. Do not throw anything in the street as dirt or stones. Pay thy respects to all thou meetest.

"With other children, do not sit upon the ground. Do not quarrel. Converse not with any but those that are good, sober and virtuous. At play, do not make thy clothes, hands or face dirty. Do not laugh at any for their natural infirmities of body or mind, but pity such as are so visited and be thankful that thou art otherwise distinguished and favored."

With such a set of rules, every child should have been perfect. But American children were growing up freer than their parents. They could be louder because houses were not built close together, as they were in the old country. There was space to run and test the lungs. A boy knew he could grow up to be whatever he wanted. Nothing except his own ignorance would keep him from earning money and owning land someday. A girl knew she would probably marry a man who owned land and that she would have some choice of whom she would marry. The book of rules was not followed everywhere in the united states.

A Pittsburgh man visited a family that he was sure had never even heard of the rule book. "The eldest boy, age 8, in the midst of dinner, whipped off my wig with great dexterity and received the applause of the table for his humor. Six of the children sat at the dinner table and entirely monopolized the wings of the fowl and the most delicate

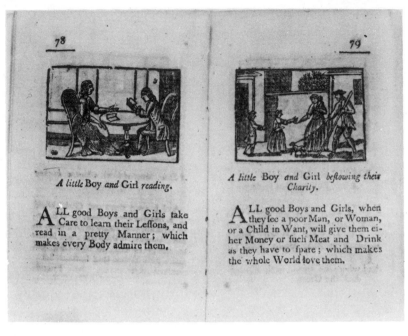

A little Boy and Girl *reading.*

ALL good Boys and Girls take Care to learn their Leſſons, and read in a pretty Manner; which makes every Body admire them.

A little Boy and Girl *beſtowing their* Charity.

ALL good Boys and Girls, when they ſee a poor Man, or Woman, or a Child in Want, will give them either Money or ſuch Meat and Drink as they have to ſpare; which makes the whole World love them.

A book that showed girls and boys how to be good and make "the whole World love them" was highly prized

morsel of every dish because the mother had discovered that her children have not very strong stomachs. In the morning, I wanted to walk upon the gravel before my friend (the father of the brood) got up. I wanted to enjoy my own thoughts without interruption, but I was followed by my little tormentors playing at what they call 'running after the gentleman.' My whip (a present from an old friend) was broken to pieces by one of the boys who is fond of horses and the handle was turned into a hobby horse. The main spring of my repeating watch was broken because the mother asked me to show it to another child."

Long before they went to school, children learned to deal with unhappiness and death as just another part of life. They took their turns, along with the adults, sitting at the bedside of a dying relative. They knew that death could come suddenly to them. They had been taught never to say, *"When I grow up . . ."* Instead, it was safer to say, "When it shall please God that I shall come to riper years . . ." or, "If it shall seem good to the Divine Providence that I arrive at manhood . . ."

Children learned early about disappointments, too, and how to get over them by working hard. One little girl had this letter from her mother, who did not live with her:

> My dear Betsey:
>   I am sorry you was so disappointed the other night. But such is our lot in life. Disappointments will come. You must learn to bear them while you are young and must learn to expect but little from the world. I am sending you some shoes to work [in needlework] for me. Only a rosebud and a few leaves upon the toe. Read your book and write me what you think of each chapter in your own words.

Masters and Pupils

Parents may not have agreed on the rules for good behavior, but they did agree on the importance of school. In Pittsburgh, Ezekiel Jones was found guilty in court of not sending his five-year-old son to school. He was sentenced to stand in a white sheet on three successive Sundays in his parish church. In the united states, any child—even Ezekiel's son—might become a future leader. Americans were very serious about teaching their children to become valuable citizens. They usually built their schoolhouse in a new town before they finished their own houses.

When children began school, the schoolmaster let the parents know he was taking over. He told the parents never to allow their children to take a holiday, except those set by the schoolmaster, and never to let their own commands be different from the master's. They must tell their children to "submit to the little imaginary hardships at school" and if they did not obey their master, they must "undergo the pain of correction." Above all, parents must never let their children tell idle tales about what happened to them in school.

For the first few years, children were terrified in school. Then they grew braver and learned which benches were broken and squeaked loudly with the smallest movement. When it came time to write in their copybooks, they made a great disturbance borrowing rulers and pencils. Older girls and boys delighted in playing tricks on the stern master. One Friday a Boston schoolteacher said, "The keys to the schoolhouse could not be found. We had to break the locks to get in. Later, we found the keys behind the rain barrel."

Sometimes even the teachers were frightened. Nathaniel Snowden was just out of the College of New Jersey (Princeton University) when he began teaching in Mr. Hunter's Latin School in New Jersey. Unfortunately, Latin had always been Nathaniel's worst subject, and some of the children knew more Latin than he did. The children played tricks on him, stuffing the heating stove with green wood which smoked up the room and helping each other with translations. Nathaniel's heart sank every time he saw two of the boys smiling at each other.

"Whenever I see the boys smiling," he said, "I think it is because of some failing of mine. My not being good in Latin leaves me open to this fault. It hurts me that I cannot run the school without beating the boys. It hurts my feelings excessively when I strike them and would almost as leave have the flogging myself."

Many grown-ups thought a teacher who did not beat the children was useless. But some teachers were cruel. While most hit the flat of a child's hand with a ruler, others bruised the child's fingertips instead. Teachers thumped their pupils on the head with their knuckles, boxed their ears, and pulled their hair. In boarding schools, punishments were more severe, because children did not see their parents often.

Dr. Benjamin Rush wrote a book to warn teachers and parents that children were being treated cruelly. He said that teachers should warn their students and keep them after school if they were bad. Or the students could be made to stand in the middle of the room, in front of the whole school, holding a small sign of disgrace. One of the worst names a child could be called was "clown." Wearing a hat like a clown's, called a dunce cap, was a hard punishment for many children.

Reading, 'Riting, and 'Rithmetic

Every day children were "ranked" in class. When the first-ranked student lost his place at the top of the class, everyone knew it, because he had to change his seat. No one worried about whether the lowest-ranked child in the class felt badly about being last. The teacher hoped he did feel very badly—then perhaps he would work harder.

Children went to "Latin schools" so they could go to college, where everyone spoke Latin. But many parents were no longer impressed with the Latin classics.

"We don't want our children learning dead languages," they said. "We want them to learn how to run a business, to speak English properly, and to learn about their own country, not ancient Rome!"

For all children, school began with the ABC's. In most schools, they learned their letters from a dreary poem in *The New England Primer* which children had been reciting for almost a hundred years!

> A In Adam's Fall, we sinned all
> B Thy life to mend, this Book attend
> C The Cat doth play and after slay

Right away, there were two new letters to learn that had not been included in the primer. The long "i" was now to be called a "jay." The sharp "u" was to be called a "vee." Then every child memorized his first poem:

> Our days begin with trouble here
> Our life is but a span
> And cruel death is always near
> So frail a thing is man.

Children did not have books. Books were too rare and expensive for a child's hands. In some schools even the schoolmaster had no books. Most adults thought a schoolmaster was not worth his salt if he had to teach from a book anyway. Instead, the schoolmaster had copybooks that he had written himself, copying the contents from a book he had seen or from his own instructor. Before school ended, each child would also own copybooks that he had made with his own hands and much sweat.

Only a few schoolteachers could afford to buy a copy of Noah Webster's Spelling Book

For very small children, the alphabet was printed neatly on a small paddle which they could carry in one hand. To keep them from smudging the letters, a piece of clear horn was laid over the letters and fastened down with thin brass strips. This "hornbook" was the closest to a reading book that some children ever owned.

The only book every child could use to practice reading was the Bible. Almost every family had one. But now, teachers said the children had heard all the Bible stories and knew all the words by heart. They could not learn to read that way. Schoolmasters were left with a big problem—how to teach reading to children who had nothing to read.

The pupils learned to write by scratching large letters on a slate with a slate pencil or chalk. They were not allowed to make small letters until they had learned how to make the large ones well. At last, one important day, they were allowed to write with a pen on a piece of paper. The big event, when they first held the quill pen in hand and dipped it into the homemade ink, turned out to be more frustrating than they had expected. First, they rubbed the paper with "pounce" to make it hold the ink better. Then they began the first letter, terrified for fear the ink would blot or the pen would skid across the paper, making the stroke go off in some awkward direction. Each letter had to be made in one sweeping motion, with upward strokes as fine as a hair and downward strokes full and black. Their letters did not look at all like the schoolmaster's. Carefully and painfully, they copied the sentences he had written:

> Remember death—think every day your last.
>
> All lazy boys obstruct their parents' joys.
>
> He who injures one threatens an hundred.

Hard arithmetic was left for "boys of the brightest genius," but all boys and girls learned the plain and practical rules of keeping daybooks and business records. Only the schoolmaster had the "sum book" with the answers, and it was homemade. The children copied the rules of arithmetic and problems to illustrate each rule into their own copybooks. In their cyphering books, they wrote:

> 4 farthings = one pence
> 12 pence = one shilling
> 20 shillings = one pound sterling
> 1 pound + 1 shilling = one guinea
> 5 shillings = one crown
> 6 shillings = one dollar

American parents wanted their children to learn about their own country. In geography class, they learned that the united states were not united at all about where each state's own borders were. One piece of land was claimed by three different states. Each of the southern states assumed that its western border was the Mississippi River. The Mississippi was called the "west coast" of the united states. The other west coast was a place that could be reached only by ship, and most of it belonged to Mexico. What was in between was completely unknown. Jedidiah Morse wrote an American geography book in 1784, but not many schoolmasters could afford to buy a copy. In it, Morse said that North America was "composed chiefly of gentle ascents" with no real mountains except for the Alleghenies and the Appalachians. Many years would go by before someone discovered the plains, deserts, Rocky Mountains, and rivers in the unknown land between the "coasts."

Lessons for Rich and Poor

Children did not study natural history, or biology, because it was in no condition to be studied. Some scientists divided all animals into two kinds: those with blood and those without. *Animated Nature,* which sounds like a natural history book, said such things as, "American bears, wolves, and elks are not able to defend themselves because they have no strong teeth or horns" and "Rattlesnakes in America make such a loud noise when they move that people can run away when they hear them coming."

Some people in the united states thought that children of poor people should not go to school. "Society cannot exist without the work that poor people do," was their argument. "Poor people were born to do that work. Who will do it if they don't? The son of a day laborer grows up knowing how to do his father's work. Having never known better things, he is contented, and sometimes even sings and whistles while he works. If he is sent to school, he will not do that work which Providence meant for him to do."

This was the way many people felt about black children —even those whose parents were free. The people often said it was hopeless to try to educate black children because they could not learn. But in New York, at the School Instituted for the Education of Negro Children, the teachers said those people were wrong. Some black children were very good in the different branches of learning and some even showed real genius. The school accepted only children nine years of age who could already spell words of one syllable. Unluckily, the school was fast running out of money.

There were also people who thought it was useless to educate girls. But from the earliest days, girls in the united states had a different future from girls in the old world. Often a girl in England did not learn to write until she was in her teens. In America, a girl was thinking of marriage by then. In frontier country or in a small town, the mother might have to educate her own children until there was a school. Everyone agreed that girls should at least learn to read, write, and be able to cipher all the arithmetic a housewife might need to know.

Young people who had reached their teens were not called "teenagers," but even then they caused their parents to shake their heads and wonder where their teaching had gone wrong. The parents blamed their worries on "young blood." Older people said, "Youth are rash while the blood runs through the veins with great rapidity. . . . Time and experience teach wisdom." One father was fast losing his patience waiting for signs of wisdom to appear in his son.

"My son's bad habits have been growing with his growth and strengthening with his strength," he said one day. "Now, in a state of manhood, they have reached the very climax of imperfection."

Fathers who could not manage their sons could send them to live with a friend far away or bind them out to learn a trade. William Nelson, a southern gentleman who raised sleek racehorses, was finally driven to write a letter to his friend Colonel Nicholas.

"My son and his friends spend most of their time galloping wherever they wish, mounted on blood horses," he complained. Nelson sent his son off to live a few years in Kentucky with Colonel Nicholas. But when he left home, the boy was riding the most indifferent nag that Nelson could find on his plantation.

Girls were in for their share of criticism, too. They were told that their health would be ruined by sitting with their legs crossed, and their morals ruined by reading novels. "It is better to be ignorant of the alphabet than to read novels," said their elders. The girls were also lectured about their old age. "A period will arrive in your life when exterior attractions will be no more. . . . You will have only your mind, so improve it now while you can."

Sons and daughters of rich people were no longer sent off to England or Europe for their education. Their parents said American boys did not learn to love their own country in foreign schools. Besides, boys who studied together in school and joined in the same sports would grow up to have ties to each other. As for the girls, parents had decided it was silly to educate them far above their fortunes. They would come home fit to marry lords and then marry an American, would have to manage their own homes and maybe even teach their own children. Girls whose parents could afford private school went off to be "finished." They learned to be good at painting, music, needlework, or any other amusement that was cultivated in the social circle they would be living in.

Not for Girls

The girl who really wanted to learn was as peculiar as if she had said she wanted to wear trousers. Girls were told never to hope for a career as a "doctoress, lawyeress, teacher of the arts and sciences, or a politician." Such fields would never be open to women. In addition, girls should remember that they were not made for "man-like action." Sports were not for women either.

The cost of private school depended on what the students learned. The Sunbury Academy in Georgia was built with money earned from selling the estates of Loyalists. Boys and girls paid 4 pounds sterling (about $13.50) a year to learn plain reading, writing, and arithmetic. For another 4 pounds 15 shillings (about $16), they also learned English grammar, geography, surveying, and navigation. Boys paid 5 pounds 10 shillings (about $18.50) to learn Latin or Greek, languages that were far too hard for the female mind to grasp. Boarding at the school cost $50 a year more. Students took their own bedding and hired someone to do their washing and bring in the firewood for warmth.

There were no high schools. Children went to primary school, then on to grammar school, if there was one and if

A boy in a private academy could learn how to speak in public

they did not have to work. This system sent many children to college at the age of fourteen.

Princeton had two schools. One was the college and the other was a lower class for the education of boys in "Grammatical Knowledge." In 1786, the college had seventy boys who each paid $100 a year to attend. The students lived and studied in a huge building four stories high, called Nassau Hall. They spoke to each other only in Latin during study hours and called each other by Latin nicknames. Animals grazed in the yard, and parts of the building badly needed repairs. The college library had been almost completely destroyed during the Revolution and an orrery, a device for studying the solar system, had been out of order since the British soldiers had used it to grind corn.

Colleges were about to become Americanized by parents who wanted their children to have something new called a "liberal education" instead of the classical one. At South Carolina College, a boy could now learn about agriculture or study the mechanic arts. In Virginia, he could attend the school of commerce, manufacturing, and diplomacy. Columbia College was one of the few colleges where a boy could study natural history, economics, or French.

There were still no books. Students learned at college by listening to lectures. When the professor asked them questions, he expected them to answer using the same words he had spoken. Exams were given orally, in front of anyone in town who cared to come. School had never been a place to have fun. Now that the young people were in college, they discovered that was not fun either. In church colleges, students were allowed no "play"—not even swimming. The only athletics at a college in Virginia were marbles and quoits.

4

Amusements and Sports

Let thy recreation be Lawful, Brief, and Seldom.
From *The School of Good Manners,* 1787

Lewis Beebe never knew that some American children had fun on a Sunday until he took a trip south.

"The children here come and go as they please!" he remarked. "After the sabbath service, the adults think it is perfectly innocent to spend the rest of the day in the company of others. They visit from house to house and drink tea."

In New England, where Beebe lived, the children that he knew spent their Sundays hearing stories about the Christian martyrs and improving their morals. A good book for Sunday recreation was *A Token for Children.* The rest of the title was "Being an Exact Account of the Conversion, Holy and Exemplary Lives and Joyful Deaths of Several Young Children." The book had been rewritten especially for New England children, who must have had mixed feelings reading, on a sunny, pleasant Sunday afternoon, about "joyful deaths" of children their own age.

Beebe was shocked. These southern families who drove about in their coaches, filled to overflowing with laughing children, would have been thrown out of his church in Connecticut for such behavior. Or worse! He had been raised to believe that anyone who played on the Sabbath risked being struck dead without warning. He himself had heard of a case where fourteen boys played ice hockey on a Sunday and the ice broke. All the boys had drowned.

But southern children had been raised far from the influences of the Puritans. They had not heard that it was wrong even to *want* to play. Southern adults were surprised when

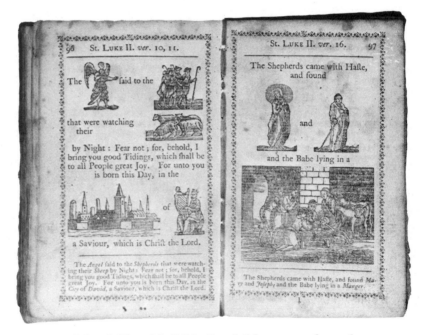

A book like this Bible for children was the only book a New England child could look at on Sunday

preachers came from New England and scolded them for finding pleasure in horse racing, playing, and laughing on Sunday.

Playing on other days of the week was all right—just so it did not look like time-wasting. Families were so large that most children had seven or eight brothers and sisters plus dozens of cousins to play with. But there were no toys. Paper and pencils were too costly to give a child who wanted to draw pictures. There were no coloring books, liquid crayons, finger paint, scrapbooks, sticky tape, or sheets of paper for budding artists. Slates and chalk had to be saved for school and were never for play.

Many children made their own toys. They made dolls from small pieces of wood or with a dried-apple head attached to a stuffed body. A boy with a Barlow knife could make checker or chess sets, darts, arrows, a chestnut whistle, a waterwheel that turned on a pin, or a "locomotive." To him, a "locomotive" was a toy that moved by itself, like a wooden animal that could walk down a sloping ramp. Boys made popguns from pieces of elder tree or small traps to catch mice. Girls were never given Barlow knives to make exciting toys. If girls clamored for something interesting to do, they were handed a piece of material to sew or a sampler to make. A girl of ten practiced making great and small letters of the alphabet with needle and thread for at least a year before she made one sampler to put her name on.

Children could make a "magical lantern" with glass sides. They painted wild animals or monsters on the glass. Then the light inside the lantern was lit and the monsters' shadows appeared against the white walls of the darkened room. When the lantern was turned slowly, the monsters moved around the walls.

Gunpowder and Games

Since gunpowder was in every American home, a boy had little trouble learning how to make air rockets, sky rockets, water rockets, fire links (fireworks that were linked like sausages), fire lances, flaming arrows, and fire wheels. The same book that taught boys how to make these lethal little toys very kindly included a paragraph on "how to make ointment for curing all sorts of burns." The book did not mention, however, that blindness or missing fingers was a very possible side effect of playing with gunpowder.

Many games were invented to use whatever equipment children had right at hand. To play Hop-Hat, the boys set their hats in a row on the ground. Each boy, in turn, hopped over the hats, one hat at a time, until he reached the last hat. This last hat he picked up in his teeth and, without turning around, tossed it from his mouth as close to the other hats as he could. Peg-Farthing was a good game for any boy who had a small piece of money and was clever with a top. One boy put his farthing into the circle drawn on the ground. If he spun the top so that it moved over and knocked the farthing out of the circle, he was allowed to keep his farthing. If not, then the next boy had a chance to knock out the farthing and pocket it. To play Chuck-Farthing, a boy had to be good at chucking his piece of money into a small hole in the ground. If he missed, the next person who threw it into the hole was the richer for it.

Other popular games were Blindman's Buff, Marbles, Knock Out and Span, All the Birds in the Air, and a more active game called Base-Ball. The 1787 version of baseball required only a few boys, since the bases were posts about three feet high. A player struck a ball with a stick, then ran to a post. He stayed there until the next player hit a ball and then the first player could move on to the next post, finally arriving back "home."

American Games

Many Americans learned new games from the Indians. Ebenezer Denny and his friend, who had been raised by the Wyandotte Indians, went to the Indian camp one day.

"We were taken very friendly by the hand and desired to fall in with them at a game of 'Common,' " said Ebenezer. Two old sachems divided the group into two equal teams. A post on each side of a decorated sugar tree marked the goal. On top of the tree was a piece of new scarlet cloth, "as much as would make a pair of leggin's" and a pair of scarlet garters.

"These were the prizes. One of the men gave a 'hollow' as a signal to make ready. It was answered by another 'hollow.' At that instant a ball was thrown up into the air. Then at it we went . . . for half an hour. At last it was sent past the post and the person who struck it last declared aloud which ended the game, he being presented with the leggin's. In the same manner the garter was played for.

"After dinner, another play called 'Mamondy' was introduced. We all sat down in a circle and two began the play with a wooden dish that had six plum stones in it, marked on each side, something like dice. They shook the dish, time about, and from certain marks one would exceed the other."

Enigmas were fun to solve on a winter night. Enigmas

were puzzles with words that had two meanings. This "Dish of Fish" appeared in a 1787 magazine, using these clues:

What most lads love to do in winter   (Skate)
A bird's resting place.   (Perch)
A pleasant drink and a married lady.   (Ale + wife = Alewife)
The 19th letter of the alphabet and
  a fashionable diversion [thing to do] (T + rout = Trout)

Every child had a few favorite rebuses—a puzzle that had only one word for an answer. Later on, when books had many pictures, rebuses were picture words. But in 1787, they looked like this:

> Three letters do compose my name.
> Backward or forward, it's the same.
> In Paradise, I once did dwell.
> So what I am, pray, ladies, tell.   (Eve)

When Books Were Scarce

Children were hungry for something to read, but there was almost nothing. The almanac, filled with jokes, household hints, and weather predictions, came once a year to the general store. City children might see a newspaper if father brought it home once a week. Almost every home had a Bible, but by the time the children could read it, many of its stories had been memorized. A few lucky children might have seen the *Children's Magazine,* which came by the post and was the size of a letter. It had stories about good and bad children—with plenty of hints so the readers would know which was which.

Bookstores sometimes sold children's books, especially in Worcester, Massachusetts, where Isaiah Thomas bought good books from England and reprinted them cheaply (and illegally) for American children. In his shop in 1786, he had

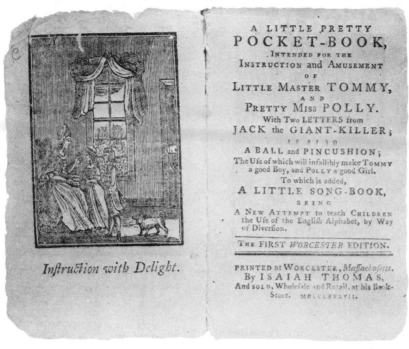

A LITTLE PRETTY
POCKET-BOOK,
INTENDED FOR THE
INSTRUCTION and AMUSEMENT
OF
LITTLE MASTER TOMMY,
AND
PRETTY MISS POLLY.
With Two LETTERS from
JACK the GIANT-KILLER;

A BALL and PINCUSHION;
The Use of which will infallibly make TOMMY
a good Boy, and POLLY a good Girl.
To which is added,
A LITTLE SONG-BOOK,
BEING
A NEW ATTEMPT to teach CHILDREN
the Use of the English Alphabet, by Way
of Diversion.

THE FIRST *WORCESTER* EDITION.

PRINTED at WORCESTER, *Massachusetts*.
By ISAIAH THOMAS,
And SOLD, Wholesale and Retail, at his Book-
Store. MDCCLXXXVII.

Instruction with Delight.

One of Isaiah Thomas' "pirated" storybooks.
Note that two presents came with it: a ball for
a boy and a pincushion for a girl

for sale *Robinson Crusoe, Roderick Random, Peregrine
Pickle, Hobby Horse, Margery Two-Shoes, The Adventures
of Master Headstrong and Miss Prudence, Be Merry and
Wise, King Pippin, Puzzling Cap, Tom Thumb's Story, Little
Red Riding Hood, Robin Hood,* several hornbooks and
geographical cards. But most parents could not afford to buy
a single book for their children.

Children who lived in the middle states and the south
could try to talk their parents into buying "chap books" from
a peddler. Chap books were filled with interesting stories—

fairy tales, ABC's, nursery rhymes, riddles, hero stories, and even shortened versions of the grown-ups' novels. But chap books did not sell in New England homes, where strict parents said the fun books served no useful purpose and would likely turn their children into "fribbles"—persons who were frivolous and thoughtless.

There were no libraries where a child could go and find a book to read. Books were so valuable that almost all libraries were "private." Only selected and approved persons could be voted into a library company and allowed to read its books by paying about $4 a year. If a father took home an interesting book, the children were not allowed to touch it unless they used "thumb papers" to keep their dirty fingers from touching the page. Philadelphia was one of the few cities with a free library where poorer people could borrow books.

At a library, men found books on law, travel, and how to tend their horses. Ladies usually asked for books on art and botany. But most ladies wanted to read novels and romances. *Power of Sympathy,* the first American novel, and *Charlotte Temple,* the first novel written by an American woman, were the favorites. Reading novels or romances was not bad because the books were racy, but only because they might give the ladies an unrealistic idea about life and fill them with romantic notions. Men were sure that women who read novels could not possibly be good wives.

The librarian had no training in how to run a library. He (or sometimes she) was made librarian because he owned a home, tavern, or store large enough to hold a stack of books. The books were shelved according to their size, not their subject matter. The only way to find a certain book was to search through the whole collection.

laughed heartily. Sirrah, faid the mafter, do you laugh at me? "No, Sir," faid the fervant, "I don't laugh at you, but I laugh to think that your horfe can't drink without a toaft this cold morning."

A foldier in time of war found a horfe. fhoe, and ftuck it at his girdle: A little after comes a bullet, and hits juft upon it. "Well," fays he, "I fee a little armour will ferve if it be well placed."

One galloping over fome plough'd land, meeting a country fellow, afked him if that was the way to *Tame*? "Yes," faid he, "to tame your horfe, if he was as wild as a buck."

Two country fellows meeting, one afked the other, "What news?" He anfwered, "He knew no other news but that he faw a very great wind laft Friday." "See a wind," fays the other: "Yes, fee it," replied he again. "Prithee, what was it like?" faid he. "Like," faid the other, "why, it was like to blow my houfe down."

A country fellow, juft come up to London, and peeping into every fhop he paffed by,

by, at laft looked into a fcrivener's; where feeing only one man fitting at a defk, he could not imagine what was fold there, and calling to the clerk, faid, "Pray, Sir, what do you fell?" "Loggerheads," cry'd the other. "Do you fo?" anfwered the countryman. "Egad! you have a fine trade then, for you have but one left."

A country farmer was obferved never to be in good humour when he was hungry, which caufed his wife to watch carefully the time of his coming home, and always

Two hundred years ago, young people enjoyed a joke book like this one

Americans really hoped to find books about their own country in libraries and bookstores, but none had been written yet. There were books on European animals, plants, and birds, but not on American ones. The only travel books were written by strangers who often made up stories about the united states, like a book called *An History of the Earth and Animated Nature,* written by a famous British writer, Oliver Goldsmith. In this book Goldsmith said, among other tall tales, "The children of negroes are able to walk at the age of two months. . . . The American earthworm is often a yard long and thick as a walking cane. . . . The pools of America abound with leeches in such numbers that it would be dangerous to go bathing there."

Sing a Rhyme

Americans in the 1780s loved poetry, but not the kind that showed how educated the poet was. Most people preferred poems that rhymed and talked about everyday things. They collected the ones from the newspapers that pleased them, like this one called "The Incurable," which begins:

> Doctor, I'd have you know I'm come
> As far as 'tis from here to home
> To tell you my condition.
> I've got the itch; I've got the gout,
> My shins are broke, I've hurt my foot,
> I need a good physician.

Singing was as popular as writing poems. The first hint that a singing school might open usually appeared in the newspaper. Young ladies and gentlemen signed up at once. They had no singing books, no printed music, no "popular" tunes, and not even any American songs to learn. The fun of going to singing school was in joining voices with the others one or two nights a week and "waiting on the girls home" after the practices. Those who could really carry a tune often moved on to join a singing society and give concerts.

Noah Webster taught a group called "The Grand Uranians." The group gave a concert one day—there were 300 singers and 400 people in the audience. But Noah was shocked when he heard a lady singing on a stage. "Very odd indeed," he said, "a woman sings in public after church for her own benefit!"

Only one or two printers in the united states had the fonts

to print music, so music books were as rare as musicians. Noah Webster played the flute, and many other people played musical instruments, but most of them would never have considered making music for a living. The most famous doctor of the day, Benjamin Rush, said that young ladies should not learn to play a musical instrument at all, because they would have to practice long hours to become good at the instrument and that was a waste of time.

Until now, the most popular musical instrument had been the harpsichord. But something about harpsichords reminded Americans of royalty and the courts of Europe. They much preferred the "forte-piano," which had a different sound. The deeper sound came from little hammers hitting the strings, instead of from strings being plucked. People who had been to Europe said a famous composer named Mozart had written many beautiful pieces especially to be played on the forte-piano. The new instruments had been sold in the united states, but they cost more than a schoolmaster earned in two years.

Moving Pictures and a Museum

People who lived in Philadelphia in 1785 could go to the "moving pictures" for 65 cents. Charles Willson Peale was a talented artist, but this was no year for an artist to live by his talent. So Peale had opened an ingenious exhibition that people called "moving pictures." The audience sat on chairs facing a small stage that looked like a picture frame. When the hall was dark, the curtain opened and the audience saw a darkened landscape. Birds sang. Dawn came and the hills, trees, and a house appeared. The music grew louder as the day became brighter. The next scene showed a Philadelphia street, the lamps lit at night and dawn coming again. Another scene showed a mill with a moving wheel and water splashing. Thunder, lightning, and rain came and went, as the Peale children supplied the sound effects backstage.

"We went to Mr. Peale's exhibition room," said Timothy Ford one day, "where all are entertained by a novel display of transparent paintings done in a masterly manner . . . but I can't pay any compliments to the music."

The following year, Peale decided the united states

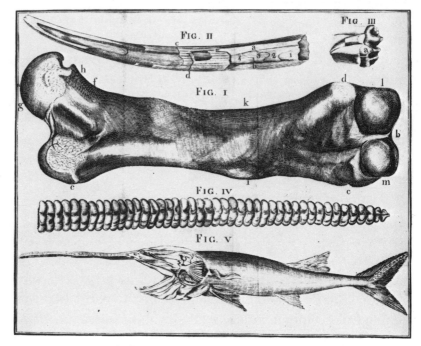

Some of the natural history curiosities in the Peale Museum included a mastodon bone, rattles from a snake, and a strange fish

needed a museum to show the newest science, natural history. Until then the closest any American had come to seeing natural history was to ogle two camels exhibited at a local tavern or the five-legged cow that attracted customers to a tavern competing across the street. Peale wanted to show Americans that natural history was really scientific, but in such a way that he could use his artistry.

He turned part of his house into a "Repository for Natural Curiosities" and invited visitors to come. Each specimen had a card telling what it was and where it had come from. At first he had an odd assortment: George Washington's stuffed pheasants, a swordfish sword that had been forced up through the bottom of a boat, a gigantic bone of an unknown animal. Then Peale made several landscapes in his rooms. He had ponds filled with stuffed fish, turtles, frogs, toads, lizards, and water snakes. On a low hill, he set up bushes filled with birds and added stuffed animals and enormous rattlesnakes. Where people had sat to see the "moving pictures" the year before, they now found a cave beside the sea filled with marine life. For the first time, Americans saw what some of the American animals looked like. They were *not,* as one European scientist had recently said, smaller and weaker than the animals in Europe.

Slightly Wicked Fun

Grown-ups who lived near one of the few cities that allowed theaters could spend an evening watching a play. New York, Philadelphia, and Charleston were almost the only cities that risked their citizens' morals with stage entertainments. In Boston, stage shows had not been allowed for forty years. By 1791, Bostoners demanded that they at least be allowed to see "such theatrical exhibitions as are calculated to promote the cause of morality and virtue."

Actors were considered such bad people that they were not even allowed to join a church. When students at Dickinson College put on a play called "High Life Below the Stairs," their professors and the college trustees were horrified. The audience loved it. In 1790, the small village of Washington, Pennsylvania, put on three plays—all the same night. The editor of the local paper wrote this the next week:

> How the Almighty is pleased with an exhibition of this nature, as it savors of the stage, I do not know . . . but it is certain his creatures were much amused, the young ladies especially.

The stage plays themselves were not half as bad as what appeared on the stage between the acts. Audiences demanded a full evening of entertainment, so when they saw a three-act tragedy, they also got a comic dance called "The Drunken Peasant" and a comedy, *The Elopement.* Even Shakespeare's *Richard III* had to share the stage with a Punch and Judy show and a man who did magic tricks. During these interludes between scenes, the comic actors often used words like "Goddam," "Bastard," "Rascal." Ladies always turned their backs to the performers during the interludes.

Seats in the theater were arranged in tiers, just as they are today, but the customers sat on benches without backs. The pit seats were the cheapest, but only women of "no social standing" would be seen there. Ladies sat in boxes which were entered by a door from the corridor. The audience was not always well behaved. One night in Charleston's Harmony Hall, the audience rioted when they were told that

At the Green Dragon Tavern, Bostoners could
see anything from a forbidden play to an Indian
treaty meeting or a traveling show with a camel

Mr. Godwin had sprained his ankle and could not dance that
night. Many of the customers shouted and threw bottles
onto the stage. One of the bottles was returned by Mr. Godwin, who limped forward swinging a sword. A number of
men jumped onto the stage, but the fight ended before
Harmony Hall was a wreck.

The number one amusement for most people south of
New England was horse racing. The Loyalists who fled during the Revolution had left behind them not only a love of
horse racing but also some very well bred horses. Races
often happened without any planning. Two horsemen met
on a street, challenged each other, and a race began from

that point to another. This happened so often in Philadelphia that the favorite street for racing was called Race Street, and it has that name to this day. In Lexington, Kentucky, settlers complained so much about the racing horses charging through the town that the town's officials had to stop racing completely. Two years later, Kentuckians built the first racetrack.

Americans wanted their races to be as respectable as those in the old country, so they had rules. Even in frontier country, the newspapers said, "No jockey shall ride without some genteel jockey habit." If any rider tried to jostle, cross, or strike another rider, his horse was thrown out of the race. Horses had to be shown and entered two days before the race. It was quite proper for ladies to attend horse races. They wore their best clothes, just as ladies in England did. Every holiday was excuse for a race. But horse racing was frowned on in New England. Preachers traveling from there through the south called horse racing a "sport" and already "sporting" was coming to mean "gambling."

"I have almost determined," said Lucy, a fifteen-year-old, "not to go to the Races this fall. Everyone appears to be astonished at me, but I am sure there is no sollid happiness to be found in such amusements. They laugh at me and tell me while I am mopeing at home, the other girls will be enjoying themselves at races and balls."

Lucy stopped writing and thought a while longer. The new preacher she had just heard was going to make her very lonely if she had to give up the races and all her Virginia friends. Then she opened her diary and, with a different color ink, started writing again.

"I am determined that I never will go to the races . . . unless I have an inclination to go."

Lucy was not alone in loving horse races. Racing was so popular that visiting and emigrant horses made the front pages of the local newspapers. When Eclipse, a high-blooded, beige stallion, came to America to sire some race horses, the newspaper published the names of all his ancestors.

"For beauty, carriage and speed, no horse on the continent excels him," said the paper. "He will be shown on market days in Philadelphia if the weather proves fine. Eclipse covered twenty mares last season, all of which are with foal except one."

Then, one day in 1788, a new horse appeared on the docks at Philadelphia. Messenger, a famous harness racer from England, brought a whole new sport to the united states. Harness racing appealed especially to this nation of travelers. They not only enjoyed the new kind of racing, but realized at once how much more comfortable travel could be if they could train their horses to trot pulling carriages, or train their riding horses to have the gentle rolling motion that a good pacer had. When Messenger died many years later, he was buried with full military honors for his service to the country.

Horses were the only means of travel, and so every village had its blacksmiths, the source of one rural amusement. A blacksmith would put a nail rod or iron bar in the ground and, in their spare time, the village men would pitch a few used horseshoes toward the bar. Pitching horseshoes was a favorite pastime for all ages, even though the game was a source of annoyance to people who didn't believe in wasting time.

The Dutch people had brought some amusements with them to New York a century before that we would call sports today. Most Americans had not liked bowling balls on the green, but bowling in a "ball alley" was becoming popular very fast. Ice-skating could hardly be called fun when the only ice skates were rusty iron runners fastened onto a shoe-size board. The board was attached to the feet with leather straps. Quite a lot of skill was required, thought Nathaniel Snowden, when he went "a-scating" on the Delaware River. The Dutch had also brought over iceboating. The 1790 version of an iceboat was not a light frame on runners like today's iceboats, but a regular sailboat with a strong plank under the hull which held two iron runners and another plank with a runner that fitted under the rudder. The heavy boat often crashed through the ice. Then it took several strong men and oxen to pull it through the thick ice and back to shore again. When a river had frozen over, many people in sleighs and wagons took advantage of the new highway to ride on, often ending their rides with a feast of roast ox, roasted right on the ice.

Swimming was more for cleanliness than for fun. After the first day in July, people went for a swim, a "bathe" as they called it, and left off their long woolen underwear. Families went to the seashore to breathe the salt air. There were bathhouses in wagons at the edge of the water, but very little actual swimming was done, because few people knew how to swim.

A "gentleman's" sport in Maryland was fox hunting. A party of ten to thirty hunters mounted their coursers, gave the signal to the hounds, and set the fox free. In the united states' version, there was no foxtail for a prize because the fox was always saved so it could be chased another day.

"The hunt makes delightful music when they pass near a field where horses are in pasture," said one traveler in Maryland who was new to the sport. "A rider could easily be thrown from his horse with his brains dashed out and the race would continue on, with only one person left behind to mark where the body had fallen."

Angling and Clubbing

Telling fish stories has always been a favorite sport, but even though fish may have been larger and more plentiful, some 1780s fish stories are hard to swallow. A Pittsburgh newspaper reported that a man was fishing in the Ohio River when he went to sleep on a high bank with his lines still in the water. Suddenly he woke to find himself bouncing down the hill, the lines twisted around his legs. When he finally managed to pull the lines in, he found he had landed a catfish 12 feet long.

"Its eyes were two feet apart," he said. Like most fish story tellers, he went on from there. He cut the fish open and found the leg of a man with a boot on, a regimental blue coat with buff lapels, and a square canteen covered with leather and filled with whiskey. He had, no doubt, sampled it well.

Merchandise stores sold fishing rods of dogwood, hickory, and red cedar, along with hair, silk, or hemp lines to use for fly, trolling, and bottom fishing. Fishhooks were hung on silk, hair, or Indian grass. Floats were made of cork and trimmed with goose or swan quills. To lure the fish to one spot, the wise fisherman made a mixture of bullock, goat, and sheep's blood. He added spices, flour, garlic, wine, suet, and marrow. Then he rolled the mixture into little pills which he scattered over the water. Crawfish could be caught with lures of goats' bowels or skinned frogs.

Golf had been a favorite sport in England and Scotland, but there is no evidence that there were golf courses in the united states in 1787. There were, however, golf clubhouses. On September 25, 1788, this notice appeared in the Charleston, South Carolina, newspaper: "There is lately erected that pleasing and genteel amusement, the Golf Baan." Dances were held there as well as anniversary parties. If the members played golf, they must have been very private about it.

How to Hunt

The most common sport in the united states was hunting. The first sports book, called *The Sportsman's Companion,* written by a "gentleman," told everything a man ever needed to know about hunting with dogs.

He advised a hunter to choose pointer pups between nine and twelve months old to train for hunting. The kinds of pointers, he said, were "the heavy Spanish dog, Russian rough dog, German dog, English dog, and the fleet dogs of England." For American country, the fleet species, with a dash of the Russian, was the best hunter.

"Choose a white dog with liver colored ears and flea bitten spots," said the "gentleman" who wrote the book. "Name it some short strong word that is easily pronounced, like Fido, Don, Dash, Flush, Ponto, Sancho."

The puppy's tail should be cut rather long, but his ears had to be cut short in the united states. This was because his ears would be torn with briers and prickly shrubs in such wild country. When his ears bled, the dog would shake his head and the blood would fly around, dirtying everybody. Dogs in England hunted in more civilized country.

"Prevent your dog from going into the street if you live in town, as they are perfect loobies and subject to many accidents," he continued.

A hunting dog should never lie close to a fire. Nor should it be allowed to chase any fowl, sheep, or cats. Its owner should train it to obey by laying down meat and not let the dog touch it. Then the dog should have to hunt for its meat before being allowed to eat it.

In the united states, said the book writer, dogs had to be trained to fetch and carry, because the country was so woodsy and filled with underbrush. Dogs in England did not have to fetch—the hunter could find the bird himself. To keep a dog from becoming "hard-mouthed" and biting down on the bird the dog was supposed to carry back to its master, hunting dogs were never to carry a bone, stick, or stone. To train a dog to fetch, the hunter made a ball of a spongy substance and stuck pins in it, with the points sticking upward, like hedgehog bristles. When the dog learned to carry the ball carefully, it would no longer bite down on birds. When it was time to take the dog into the field, the trainer put a collar on the dog's neck with nails driven through it. If the dog tried to spring on a bird, the nails would prick its neck.

At last came the day to hunt. The "gentleman writer" told the hunter to set out with a friend in a two-horse chair, with another chair for the servant. (No gentleman ever traveled without a servant—even in the wilds of the united states.) The servant carried the dogs, provisions, and ammunition. The cost would be well over $10 a day, not counting the powder and shot. Gentlemen always took turns at the shooting, so each knew what he had hit. And they always walked with their guns uncocked, muzzles high, so they didn't shoot each other.

After all the instructions, the "gentleman" set off for Long Island's brushy plains to try out his own luck at shooting American grouse. He took with him a Spanish dog named Bullhead.

"Bullhead jumped all over, yelping," he complained. After a scolding, Bullhead got worse. The dog scared all the birds away from the area and the hunters had to move to another place. This time, the "gentleman" tied Bullhead to the servant's waist with a bell on the rope.

"When I fired, Bullhead took off and pulled the man with him, trailing him headfirst through the brush."

The servant had to cut the rope to get free. Bullhead spent the rest of the day at a great distance. The birds were long gone from the place.

"If Bullhead had been my dog," said the "gentleman," "I would have shot him."

5

YOUNG LOVE AND EARLY MARRIAGE

Oh Celia, let the busy fly
Still hum its mazy round;
'Twill drown the murmur of a sigh
In lover's bosom sound.
> From "Poem on a Lady Striking
> a Fly with her Fan,"
> in *American Magazine*, 1787

In her father's parlor, pretty Rebecca Slater carefully poured tea for her father's guests. She choked back the lump in her throat. The guests had been careful not to say anything that would upset her, but she knew what they were thinking.

Her life was ruined. Just a few months ago, she had been a happy bride. Now she was so poor she did not even own the dress she was wearing. Her father had bought it.

Rebecca had married a handsome young foreigner. He was well educated. His manners were perfect. Their honeymoon had been a blissful sail to Europe. Soon after they arrived, Rebecca had stepped out of her coach one day to discover that her young husband had been thrown into a debtor's prison and was not likely to leave it for many years.

There was nothing Rebecca could do to help him. She could not work to pay off her husband's debts, because her education had trained her to do nothing more than be a decoration in a home. She could not divorce her husband. She could never remarry unless he died. She was a pauper, living in her father's home. Rebecca Slater was trapped. One of the guests at tea that day wrote her story in his diary after he went home.

In the old world, parents often coaxed their young people into an "arranged marriage." But that had never worked in the united states, where boys and girls insisted on choosing their own mates. Parents planted ideas about choosing the right husband or wife in their children's minds through all the years they were growing up. Then, when they reached the "courting age," the parents had ideas on how to bring two young people together, even though they managed to make the meeting look accidental.

Choosing a Mate

First, a young man was invited to "take a dish of tea" with a respectable older couple who just happened to have a visiting niece (cousin, friend, sister). After meeting a young man at tea, it was perfectly proper for a girl to invite him to a dance given that week. It was also considered fair for a young man to notice a pretty girl, track down someone who knew her family, and wangle his own invitation to tea.

Seated stiffly around the tea table, the young couple barely spoke to each other. Tea table conversation was supposed to include everyone and be about safe subjects such as the weather, concerts, or books (but never novels). Many budding romances never got past the tea table stage.

"Miss Beckwourth has a brilliancy of understanding—far above even the improved part of her sex," said Timothy Ford. "She can talk on any subject."

But Timothy had met another young girl at the tea table that day. "I confess I am rattled by the disposition of Miss Smith," he said later. "She has a great flow of spirits . . . talks a great deal without saying anything . . . and uses profane words like 'Oh God!' that would sound better coming from the mouth of a sailor!" Timothy invited Miss Beckwourth to a sleigh ride.

Girls were in no great rush to get married. Their fathers had ruled them all their lives, sometimes very strictly. When they married, they would just be trading one lord and master for another one. At least they knew what their fathers were like.

A girl was always very formal, never calling a boy by his first name in public. Even in the privacy of a diary, the girl referred to her boyfriend as "Mr. B." or perhaps "Mr. Beal." Later, after she married, she still called him "Mister" in front of her friends. But the boys were not so formal. In their diaries, a girl friend became "my heart," "the most lovely," and "my fair one."

Boys complained that the girls flirted too much, were often vain, and fell into a "pet" when things did not go their way. Girls complained that boys were not perfect either. Elizabeth Cranch spent one evening with a boy who really annoyed her.

"Must flattery be a part of every young man who aims to please," she complained as she shut the door behind him. "I

Amelia and other novels were the soap operas
of the day

cannot be at ease with this young man. He is so forward and says so much with so great a share of confidence that I am bashful."

Sharing confidences and being frank with each other was not a part of courtship. Instead, the couple played a sort of game to keep each other ignorant of personal feelings. Eliza told James that she was reading a racy novel. She knew very well that he did not approve of girls who read novels.

"What novel?" James asked.

"Emily Montague," said Eliza.

"I do not approve of novel reading," said James stiffly.

"Neither do I," said Eliza, wondering if she had gone too far. "I only read them for enjoyment."

"Then," James said sternly, "you are not always guided by your better judgment. You cannot take the trouble to oppose your inclinations."

Soon after this argument, James left to go home. He wondered whether Eliza was a good candidate for a wife or not. She wondered whether James was as stuffy as he seemed.

Subtle (?) Hints

When a girl did not want to encourage a boy's attention, she went about it in a hundred subtle ways.

"I went to pay a visit to the sisters," said James Gibson one day. "Leonora was very industrious with her needles, but Rachel devoted herself to entertain me." Hint number 1: Leonora isn't interested. Rachel is.

Lewis thought he had met the lady of his dreams in Maryland, but she told him that she could never marry anyone

who asked her to leave her state. "Then she told me," said
Lewis, "it was unusual to permit a man to kiss her hand after
only a year's acquaintance." Hint number 2: Lewis was wasting his time.

But when subtle hints failed to hit home, the girls knew
how to throw out stronger clues. Nathan Webb was the
target when he went to pay a call on his friend Matilda.
"There was another man there," Nathan said sadly. "I was
as welcome as water in a newly launched ship."

Young men and women did not always know much about
each other when they married. George Nelson was middle-
aged and happily married to his second wife when he happened to travel through the town where his first wife was
buried. He thought it would be nice to visit her grave. But
she had a surprise waiting there for him on the tombstone
that he had never seen. Eight years after she had died he
discovered that she had been fifty years old on the day they
were married. George had only been twenty-five!

While looking around for the right girl to marry, the boys
were not always shy. Before Noah Webster met his Miss
Greenleaf, he had admired dozens of girls. When a doctor
told him his eyes were too weak to study, he answered that
if he could not devote his time to books, then he would
devote it to the ladies. And he did. He went to a Friends'
meeting one day to worship. Coming home, he said, "I was
very attentive . . . to the silent worship of a pretty girl of
sixteen. Such blushes, such lips, make one feel devotion."

One of the busiest young men was Daniel Mulford. Daniel
had no hang-ups about getting acquainted fast or waiting a
year to kiss a lady's hand.

"Elizabeth is full of radical heat," he reported. "Sallie, two
years younger, is far more reserved but is better in good

sense. Nancy and Polly, the twins, are scarcely halter broke, for such is the quality of mares in their village that colts are not rid till they get their full strength. Susan is in all respects agreeable. I think I am a little twisted by her. Went on a visit to a Mr. Goodwin's. We spent a merry afternoon and, in the evening when kissing games could be introduced, the girls got pretty well gnawed."

Most young men did not have Daniel's talent in playing parlor games. An evening spent in the company of young ladies usually included nothing more exciting than watching the girls do fancy needlework or playing cards. And how did the girls think of the young men? After a more or less dull evening Anna and Maria Bancroft could not even remember their names.

"We were visited by a number of candidates," said Anna. "We played cards with two of them who went home at 11 o'clock."

Problems of Being a Girl

Girls were not chaperoned, unless brothers, sisters, parents, and servants walking past the parlor door counts. Every boy lived for the moments when he could get his girl out of the house. In the winter there was sleigh riding. A company of twenty or thirty young people all dashed off to a tavern several miles away, where they warmed up with hot chocolate—never anything stronger. The only risk in a sleigh ride was that the snow might turn to rain during the evening, and the sleigh could not get back without snow. When that happened, the young men had to rent a carriage to deliver the ladies home. Hayrides took the place of sleigh rides in warmer climates.

In the south, no one who had money spent a holiday such as Thanksgiving or Christmas in the city. Outside Charleston, South Carolina, city people had country homes bulging with frisky young guests. The rice had been cut and stacked high in the barns. The same young ladies who had been so prim and prudish in the parlor now behaved like birds uncaged, perching on the tall stacks of rice. They tumbled down merrily when the boys climbed up to join them and the stacks collapsed. When the boys went hunting, the liberated girls ranged through the plantations and barnyards, flushing out the game for the boys to shoot. At night there were dances—sometimes as far away as a two-hour carriage ride.

In the summer, a company of young people went off to gather huckleberries or some other fruit. Putting the huckleberries in their buckets was only half the sport. Daniel Mulford tells about the other half.

"After throwing huckleberries about half an hour, Semantha and I took our distance to fight a duel. We sat on the ground about three feet apart and fired single berries. She aimed at my head and I at her heart. Several of my shots entered, at least I saw them roll beneath her kerchief. [Semantha evidently wore a "modesty piece" at her neck, but it was not overly modest.] She, with a stout heart and bold face, was willing to continue in the firing as long as I pleased."

After a while, a boy began wondering more seriously about marriage, especially after he thought he had found the right girl. His married friends had been telling him for a long time that being a bachelor was no fun. "Bachelors never get rich" was a vulgar saying. Thomas Nelson wrote to tell his best friend what he should do when he got depressed.

"You certainly have the Hippo sometimes," he said. Having the Hippo was the same as having the blues. "If you have it now, mount your little chestnut mare and gallop away to some acquaintance's house where there are a parcel of pretty girls and chat with them for an hour or two. You old bachelors are strange beings. Why don't you get a wife? The many solitary hours you must pass!"

The reason many boys did not marry sooner was money.

"I thought I couldn't afford to marry either," said one young man after five years of being married. "But in the fascination of love, I ventured to try the experiment. I discovered that either I earn more money by paying more attention to business or I am spending less in useless amuse-

A winter sleigh ride often ended with hot chocolate in a tavern and a dance

ment, or else my wife saves money better than I did as a
bachelor."

Since a girl could not come right out and ask a man if he
made enough money to marry her, this delicate job was
usually handled with great tact by her father.

"How much money do you make?" Mr. Greenleaf asked
Noah Webster.

"Well, sir . . . ," Noah answered, stalling for time. (Could
the writer of the dictionary have been at a loss for words?)
"I have just published my Grammatical Institutes, and—"
Noah hesitated, and then brightened a little, "and I have
been giving my lectures on Grammar in the south."

"Were you paid well for the lectures?"

"Oh yes, sir," Noah answered truthfully. "Many persons
paid one dollar each to attend."

"I understand you had only six in the audience at Williamsburg," said Mr. Greenleaf, not unkindly.

Noah blushed. "I imagine that was because I was a stranger and a yankee, sir, although I was well introduced. The
Virginians seem to have little money and great pride. They
don't understand grammar."

Mr. Greenleaf felt as badly as Noah. But he was not going
to trust his beloved daughter to the keeping of a man who
earned his money (and precious little money at that) by
writing.

"You should get a job teaching," he told Noah.

Noah knew the subject was closed. He had asked for the
hand of Miss Greenleaf and the answer was not "yes." Neither was it "no." He went to Philadelphia's Episcopal Academy, where he was a schoolmaster for half a year and hated
every minute of it. But he did win Miss Greenleaf eighteen
months later. Ten days before he married, Noah was still

promising himself to "leave writing and do more lucrative business." Luckily for users of Webster's Dictionary (which he had not yet written), Noah did not keep to his resolution.

"A good wife," said a magazine in 1787 "should be like three things that she should not be like. Like a snail, she should keep within her own house, but unlike a snail, she should not carry everything she owns on her back at one time. Like an echo, she should speak only when spoken to, but unlike the echo, she should not try to have the last word. Like the town clock, she should always be on time, but unlike the clock, she should not speak loud enough for all the town to hear."

When a young man was ready to marry, the advice he heard most often was, "You can make only one mistake." There was no divorce. In the south, where the Church of England was the strongest church, unhappy couples could supposedly get a divorce in a "bishop's court." The catch was that there was no bishop's court in the united states. The Constitution allowed each state to grant divorce, but the process was so long and involved that only a few persons ever managed to get one.

Couples who could not live together separated. But separation was almost impossible for a female unless her father allowed her to return home and gave her clothes to wear. The children belonged to their father. The mother could not take them with her or even have them to visit. The separated wife could not work to support herself because all the money she earned belonged legally to her husband.

Very few jobs were open to women anyway. An educated girl could open a "school for young ladies." An uneducated one could open a boardinghouse for children who went to a school in the town. But both of those jobs involved having money—or at least a house. A woman could be a nurse for someone else's child, a servant, or a seamstress.

Wives had no possessions of their own. They did not even own the clothes on their backs. Everything belonged to their husbands. When one woman went to court to find out if she could make a will, the verdict was that since she could not have anything to leave anyone, she should not be allowed to make a will.

When a man died, he often left his wife all her clothing and "loaned" her the house she was living in for her lifetime. When Thomas Nelson died in 1789, he left his wife "her jewels and a chariot with four horses to hold as her own proper goods forever." In addition to "loaning" her the house, he also "loaned" her the slaves who lived there, the utensils, and the freedom to cut firewood from some land he owned.

When a girl inherited money from her father, the money became her husband's as soon as she married. He could do whatever he wished with it. One husband spent all his wife's money and then was unable to work because he became sick. His wife had to have his permission to go out to work to support him and the children. And then she had to give the money to him. The only way a wife could keep any money for herself was to take charity from her friends or keep a business under a false name.

Knowing all this did not make it any easier for a girl to choose a partner. For Noah Webster, something else made the choice hard. "If there were but one pretty girl in town," said he, "a man could make a choice. But among so many, one's heart is pulled twenty ways at once. The greatest difficulty, however, is that after a man has made his choice, it remains for the lady to make hers."

After a girl married, she would have to be happy living where her husband chose to live, even though he might like the country and she might hate it. If there was not enough money for him to enjoy his "innocent pleasures," she was supposed to cut down on her own expenses. She even had to say good-by to her own best friends and take on her husband's friends, whether she liked them or not.

This last was hard not only on the young wife, but on her best friends. Lucinda had two best friends, Polly and Hannah. When Hannah married, Polly and Lucinda were thrilled. They wore new dresses and dropped flower petals in Hannah's path on the way to church. But a few weeks later, Lucinda wrote a sad letter to her friend Polly.

"I am afraid Hannah thinks of nothing but her new husband. You can't think how dejected she always is in his absence! You may depend on it, Polly, this said Matrimony alters us mightily. I am afraid it alienates us from every one else. It is, I fear, the bane of female friendship. Let it not be with ours, My Polly, if we should ever marry."

A Serious Business

But there were deeper worries for a girl when she married. She knew that marriage was sure to be followed by babies. About every two years she would have a baby, until someday she had ten or twelve little ones. Each time she had a baby, the mother knew she might die. Many mothers took fevers and died. No one knew what caused them. A mother also knew that some of her babies would die. Almost half the babies born never lived to be six years old. To add to her worries, there were even husbands who changed their affec-

Sanguine · Choleric

tions. But surely, each girl thought, my husband will not do that if I make his home a pleasant one.

About the only thing that worried a young man on his wedding day was whether or not he would be happy. On October 26, 1789, Noah Webster said, "This day I became a husband. I have lived a long time a bachelor. . . . I am united to an amiable woman and if I am not happy, shall be much disappointed."

From the looks of the wedding announcements in newspapers and magazines, just about everyone married "an amiable woman." Abraham Kirkpatrick married "the amiable Miss Mary Ann Oldham." Another man married "a lady possessed of every amiable quality," and a Charleston man married "a young lady endowed with every accomplishment to render the marriage state happy."

A girl took a chance when she chose a husband
—he could turn into any of these four types

Weddings were not large-scale productions. There was no
parade of bridesmaids, ushers, flower girls. No organ music,
no three-layer cakes with bride and groom on top, no flowered altars, no ribbons down the aisle, not even a large party
afterward. The bride was too practical to wear a wedding
dress that could not be worn for several years afterward. She
did often keep the color a secret, though, until the big day.

Weddings were usually held at home for just a few friends
and relatives. Other friends were invited to call and meet
the new couple later. The only obligation that newlyweds
had was to be "at home" for the next few days so their
friends could come to call. Elizabeth Bancroft called the day
after the wedding to see her friend Nancy, feeling almost as
if her friend had died. "This morning," said Elizabeth
gloomily, "she is no more Nancy Lawrence, but Nancy Far-

rar. May peace and happiness attend her."

Peace and happiness did not attend all married couples. Some of those amiable young ladies and their gallant young men turned out not to be so perfect after all. Every city's newspaper had announcements like these on the back page:

> Elizabeth hath eloped my bed and board. Gone off with Leonard, well-set, 5′8″, bushy hair, has a somewhat sleepy look. He has a wife and family. Loiters in taverns; pretends he was a wagon master, but he was only a wagon driver.

> Isabella Culbertson ran off with John Deary. They stole a canoe and went down river.

> Run away last night my wife, Bridget Coole. She is a tight, neat body, and has lost one leg. She was seen riding behind the Priest of the Parish, and as we never was married, I will pay no debt she does contract. She lisps with one tooth and is always talking about Fairies, and is of no use but to the owner, Phelim Coole.

Not many disappointed husbands were able to turn their tragedy into a poem, however, like Dennis O'Bryan.

> July the 27th day, my wife Betty ran away
> From bed and board did flee and say
> She would no longer with me stay.
> That she may see her error,
> When I live happy with a Fairer . . .
> Therefore I forwarn, both great and small
> To trust her anything at all
> For her contracts from this day,
> Not one farthing will I pay.

6

How We Made Money

When I of money am possessed
The world to faults is blind.
By every man I am caressed;
No foes on earth I find.
From *Pittsburgh Gazette,*
April 1787

Hugh Ross owned land on the river across from the small town of Pittsburgh, Pennsylvania. Suddenly the little town was becoming "the gateway to the west." Hundreds of people stopped there before they went down the Ohio River to Kentucky and other frontier country. Hugh decided he could make some money if he built a ferryboat.

"You can't do that!" shouted a man who already owned a ferry. "You don't have authority to run a ferry."

"I fought for the liberty of this state," argued Hugh. "I don't need authority from anyone to start a ferry. This is a free country."

That day, the other ferry owner learned about free enterprise and the new American way of doing business. He had a piece of paper to show that his ferry had been approved by the Crown. Now it meant nothing. If he wanted to keep on running his ferry, he would have to compete for business with Hugh Ross. Instead, he tried to buy Ross's property. When that did not work, he tried to prove that Ross did not own his land legally. After that failed, he put a fence across the road so travelers could not reach Ross's ferryboat landing.

Meanwhile, Hugh had some ideas about competition, too. He built a tavern where customers could wait in comfort for

The view from Bushongo Tavern overlooks the highway to Baltimore. Note how narrow the bridge is compared to the road

the ferry. He charged threepence (instead of the fourpence the other man charged) to carry a man, a horse, or a load.

"It's absurd," said Hugh, "for one man to have the exclusive privilege of running a ferry. Especially after the struggle for which so many brave and virtuous citizens suffered."

Hugh's line of customers grew, especially on Sundays, since he allowed all foot passengers to cross the river free on the Sabbath days when there was a minister preaching in Pittsburgh. But since there was no full-time minister there yet, Hugh did not lose much money on that deal.

A Mess of Money

Money was never in a worse mess. There were English pounds and shillings, Spanish dollars, French money, and American dollars in circulation. Some states made their own money, which was worthless in other states. Some people made their own money, and it was worthless everywhere.

"What's *that?*" asked a pretty young woman who was collecting the fares from passengers on the ferry between New Jersey and New York.

"It's a copper half-sou," said a passenger angrily. "It's perfectly good money, coined by the Assembly of New Jersey."

"Well, I don't give a hoot for the Assembly of New Jersey," answered the fare taker. "Their members are no better than I am and they can't make me take their money." The passenger had to dig through his pockets to find money she would accept.

People felt the same about paper money. One day the shopkeepers in Newport, Rhode Island, refused to take paper money from customers. The law said that the merchants had to take the paper money—or else. They decided on the "or else" and closed their shops. Their customers rioted and broke the shops open.

Nobody trusted paper money. It was even blamed for spreading smallpox. In 1786 a magazine editor asked an educated man to write an article on money for the magazine. He wrote: "Money is money—and Paper is paper."

For someone to lend another person one hundred silver dollars and be paid back with one hundred paper dollars was unthinkable! One reason people did not trust paper money was that it could be cut. Sometimes people cut a paper dollar into four equal parts and said that each fourth was worth 25 cents. But some people cheated. They cut their dollar bills into three pieces. They kept the middle piece and passed off the two end pieces as "half dollars." Later, they claimed the middle piece was a "half dollar," too.

Henry Wismer did not trust any paper bills. For reasons of his own, he carefully marked all the paper money that passed through his hands, then wrote down what he had done in his account book:

> My forty Doler bill is marck with a tick in the H of Hall on the back side and a tick with the pen at the Rute of the big flower on the back side and a tick in the midel of the litel flower and a tick in the Y of Forty.

> Isack Hills 38 dolers bill is markt in the 6 for 8 dolers with a tick and one 6 doler bill marckt in the H for Hall with a tick.

> The woman at David Steevins 4 Doler bill is marckt in the D for Doler on the back side.

Copper coins were almost as much a problem as the paper money. In 1787, twenty-one coppers were worth a shilling in New York. Naturally, a good many of these showed up in Philadelphia, where a person only had to give fifteen coppers to get a shilling. The same year, federal cents (called coppers) were coined in New York. They said "Mind Your Business" on them. Halfpennies were made in Greenwich, England, with the eye of Providence and thirteen stars on one side. Most shopkeepers did not care how impressive a coin looked. They relied on biting coins to taste the copper and weighing coins to be sure they were not cheated.

Disaster Survival

People who owed money in those days were not able to pay their debts. In the old days, British soldiers would have put them in debtor's prison. But a man could never pay his debts if he went to prison. Everyone hoped that a better way would be found soon. Meanwhile, businessmen, like Thomas Clifford, had a terrible time collecting the money that people owed them. When Clifford called on a man to collect his money, the man would answer, "Of course, I will pay you at once, but first I must collect the money that Mr. Smith owes me." Then the man would send his servant on a week's journey to find Mr. Smith and collect the money owed. Mr. Smith, of course, pulled the same trick when the servant arrived. Somehow, Clifford never did get his debts collected.

Clifford had been a trader and made his living importing goods from England. Before the war, wealthy people had bought everything they needed from England—from teapots, chariots, and biscuits to black-marble tombstones. They sent their watches to England to be repaired. Millers bought grindstones from there.

But now the importing business was not what it had been.

Many states forbade their citizens to buy goods from England. In other states, Americans were not getting what they had ordered from overseas. One rich man was insulted because he had ordered material for trousers, and his shop in England had sent him jeans material. "Jeans material is for people who labor!" he said angrily. A housewife wrote an angry letter to "Messrs Farrar and Garrat, Earthenware Men" saying they had sent the worst assortment of teapots, milk pots, brown mugs, she had ever seen.

A man who had tried to import some shoes to sell wrote: "Mr. Davis's calamanco shoes are so unreasonably large that they will fit none but a country girl who has been accustomed to go barefoot from childhood." But the most surprised importer was a merchant from Wilmington, North Carolina, who had ordered 30,000 black tacks. He received a letter back from England apologizing. "We have rummaged through London, Birmingham, and Sheffield," said the note, "and have been able to come up with only 10,000 *blackjacks,* but we may be able to send more later."

Thomas Clifford wrote his wife that he did not know what to do. Americans were starting to make their own products in their own factories.

"The people here are raising and manufacturing almost every article that the country wants," he said sadly. "New Jersey is manufacturing white linen. The stock of wool is increasing. A variety of articles are made in the Iron way— almost the whole of their nails and other heavy articles. Some glass houses are getting to work and so fewer people will buy Bristol glass [made in England]. If I am not mistaken, this country will soon be in a situation to pay all it owes if peace and harmony should prevail."

The news that was so very bad for Thomas Clifford was the

best news in the world for the united states. Business was starting to boom. Men and women stopped wearing imported clothing. A stocking manufacturer announced that he was putting Americans on a proper footing with his neat worsted stockings that he made "not so thick as before." Mr. Knight Dexter donated ten acres of land in Providence, Rhode Island, to anyone who would build some sort of factory on it.

Inventors had ideas, but they had to eat. There was no money to encourage them. A man named Arthur Donaldson invented a machine called the "Hippopotamus" that dredged around docks and raised sand from the river bottom, which was used for making mortar. Another man named John Fitch claimed that he had "a machine of infinite value to the united states" called a steamboat. James Rumsey announced he had designed a "motor" boat.

Thomas Clifford was right. Only two years later, Americans proved they could make almost everything they needed. A shoe factory made 70,000 pairs of women's shoes. A prize was offered for the best American-printed books, but every part of the book had to be made in America. At least four glass factories were making glass. So many silkworms were being raised in Connecticut that soon it would be patriotic for men to wear silk stockings and for ladies to have silk dresses again. American blistered steel was almost as good as the English steel.

Even though business was better, stores in the country and on the frontier gave no credit. They had signs that read:

Cheap, ready-money store
where
NO CREDIT WHATEVER
will be given.

In the west, stores allowed barter instead of money. A person who wanted to buy salt which cost 7½ shillings a bushel could either pay cash or pay in prime furs like mink, raccoon, muskrat, beaver, or wildcat. The salt cost a little more, however, when it was paid for in bearskins, deerskins, beeswax, hemp, bacon, butter, or beef cattle. It cost even more when paid for with country produce like vegetables.

The fur trade was doing well, especially now that the ladies in England were all carrying giant fur muffs. Traders hoped that American ladies would not want to follow the same fashion, because they could make much more money sending the furs to England. The traders made fun of the fashion of muffs here, calling them "hairy comforters."

One reason why the fur-trading business was so profitable was that the trapper, who lived in the woods, needed very little. He was paid practically nothing for his work, except some flour and whiskey. The middleman made all the money from this load of furs brought in by just one trader between July 6 and 10 in 1786 in Pittsburgh:

2173 summer deer skins	29 fox skins
74 fall deer skins	419 muskrat skins
48 fawn skins	29 fishers
94 bear skins	14 martens
37 elk skins	15 wild cat
84 beaver skins	17 wolves
278 raccoon skins	16 panthers

and 67 pairs of "mockisons"

Farmers were not doing well. In the east, many farmers tried to grow corn every year in the same field, and each year the corn grew smaller.

"You should rotate your crops," the American Philosophical Society told farmers. "Grow corn one year in the field and grow beans or another crop the next year. Then your soil will not wear out."

The Philosophical Society was made up of the country's best scientists. In those days, "philosophical" meant "scientific." Science was not taught in colleges, and "scientists" were only rich amateurs who could afford to experiment with new ideas. This society of learned men collected scientific information from everywhere in the world so they could bring useful knowledge to the new united states.

The "swallow" or pit at Sinking Spring Valley
was one of the oddities that tourists reported to
the American Philosophical Society

Their president was Benjamin Franklin and their building was beside the State House in Philadelphia.

Some of the new ideas that scientifically-minded men sent to the Philosophical Society were about farming and manufacturing. People wrote about meteors, unusual caves, sinking springs, and waterfalls they had found. Some wrote about a new way to rescue people from the third floor of a burning house. One scientist sent a list of all the plants grown in foreign countries that could be raised easily in the united states.

One of these plants was a new kind of cotton. The cotton planted before the Revolution was not very good. Southerners tried Sea Island or smooth-seed cotton and it was better. Plantation owners were all excited over Bahama cotton and found it was the best so far.

One reason why few people planted cotton was that there was no way to turn it into cloth. The British government had been very careful to see that no machines for making textiles ever came to the new world. They had known very well that if the colonists ever learned how to manufacture their own cloth, they would not have to buy it from England. The English not only did not allow machines to be shipped to the new world, they did not even allow a mechanic who had worked on the machines to leave England.

The blacksmith had one of the most important jobs in the country

A Mill from Memory

But one young man of twenty-one, Samuel Slater, slipped by the British emigration officer. Samuel had grown up in England near a factory that made stockings. His father knew the factory owner and, when Samuel was fourteen years old, arranged for the boy to become an apprentice there. Samuel was a natural mechanic. He was so thrilled with the huge Arkwright machine that made the stockings that he even spent all day Sunday, his only day off, looking at it.

No one realized that Samuel had a photographic memory. His brain was storing up a picture of what that machine looked like just as if he had diagrams on paper in front of him. When his apprenticeship was over, Samuel was a mechanic. But he knew he wanted to make money and it could not happen in England. He also knew that, because he was a mechanic, he could not go to the united states. So he told the customs agent that he was a farmer, and sailed in 1789.

One year later, Samuel built an Arkwright machine from memory. Before Christmas in 1790, the first cotton mill began working at Pawtucket, Rhode Island, with Samuel in charge. Soon every general store in every little country town had cotton cloth.

In the country, there were not many ways to make money outside of farming. A clerk earned $300 a year; the schoolmaster $200. A husband and wife might run a general store, with a little fur trading as a sideline. A merchant who liked the outdoor life might try peddling. Peddlers carried their stores on their backs, packed in two oblong tin trunks. They walked or rode horseback, taking their country customers all sorts of "Yankee notions" like a "machine" to remove cores from apples, a handy-shaped tin pan, bone-handled forks, or a local cure for sore feet. Peddlers often carried bark, roots, or other "cures" from one village to another. For children, they carried chap books, filled with happy stories and fairy tales that strict New Englanders would not allow in the house.

Every country village had its cowherd, sheepherder, and calf keeper, who led the animals out to feed by day and locked them into their pens at night. Farmers cut their initials or some other identifying mark into the ears of their own animals. Every village also had a hogreeve, whose job it was to keep track of the hogs which roamed freely through the streets eating the garbage that was thrown out at night. In Philadelphia, the cowherd blew his horn as a signal for people who owned cows to turn them out into the road. Then he created an early version of a rush hour traffic jam leading the cows to pasture south of the city each morning and home each night.

City Shopping

City people called country people "rustics" and made fun of them in their jokes. City people did not have to make their own clothing. They could go to a tailor. They could buy medicines at the apothecary shop. The city's main street had every kind of shop they needed.

The apothecary shop was the place to buy medicine, although most housewives had favorites at home that they used first. If a doctor talked them into trying his favorite prescription, they went to the apothecary shop. Unfortunately, prescriptions were always written in Latin and very few apothecaries could read Latin. They rarely weighed the drugs they put into medicines. They liked to measure them by hand and eye. If the apothecary did not have all the ingredients the doctor asked for, he substituted others. For a patient with whooping cough, the apothecary sold sugar plumbs at about $1.25 a box. He had dozens of drops, pills, lozenges, and bottled brews that "cured" anything.

At the hatter's, a man could still buy a beaver hat, but they were going out of style. Most men had replaced their old three-cornered hats from Revolutionary War days with the new "round" hat. Women all seemed to want broad chip hats of straw, like the one worn by the female preacher, Jemima Wilkinson.

The Spinning Wheel owned by John Keene in Philadelphia was like the merchandise stores in every city. Here customers could buy material of every sort to take to a tailor or seamstress. Material had names like calamanco wool (with checks on one side), cassimere wool, plush, prunellas, calico, and chintz. Ladies could buy shawls called mantuas, lace, ruffles, rustles, flowered hankies, and something called "non-so-pretties" (underwear). In addition, Keene sold buttons, ink powder, pots, skillets, brass candlesticks, window weights, and bags of filberts and almonds.

Shoppers went to the stationery store to buy paper and the newest books. They could also find black lead pencils, pocket memo books made of ass's skin, penknives, sealing wax to close their letters, quills, the almanac, slates and slate pencils, English playing cards, and something called "Irish wafers." The wafers came in pink, azure, lilac, and pea green for young men and ladies, and in red for serious businessmen. Although they were made of wheat because paper was still very expensive, they were not for eating. Wafers were calling cards. A person never went to visit another person without leaving behind a calling card to say he or she had been there.

Taverns, Tailors, and Tinkers

A tavern was not to be confused with an alehouse. People got drunk in alehouses. Taverns were high class. Stage-coaches stopped at taverns and so they were often filled with travelers and important people. Local people went to the tavern to pick up their mail, read the newspaper, conduct their business, and meet their friends. Since a tavern was usually the only large building in a new town, it was used for everything from church meetings and elections to a brain operation performed before an audience by a country doctor.

Very little clothing was already made. City folk went to a tailor like Philip Thompson to have nice clothing made. Thompson made "Ladies' riding habits in that neat and genteel fashion so much admired by the most celebrated huntresses in Europe." Tailors did all their sewing by hand and worked surprisingly fast. Nathan Webb bought some sheepskin leather for less than $1 and took it to a tailor to be made into a pair of trousers. The trousers were finished the next day and Nathan paid the tailor 27 cents for his work.

At the upholsterer's, shoppers went to buy bed curtains, window curtains, feather beds, mattresses, carpets, traveling trunks, cots, hammocks, sacking for bed bottoms, stuffed "sophas," and chairs. Of course the upholsterer did not have these items already made in his store. He made them to order. At the ironmonger's, shoppers bought things made of iron: knives, stirrups for saddles, hinges, locks, and tools.

A seaport city had something called a "military store." There, the captain of a privateer could outfit his ship with rammers, sponges, sheepskins, round and double-headed cannon shot, musket and cannon cartridges, cartridge boxes, cutlasses, boarding pikes, poleaxes, grape shot already made up, match rope, iron nails, powderhorns, handcuffs, lanthorns, messkits, lampblack (to cover faces at night), and coffeepots. This kind of business was slow, but would soon pick up again. Many ship captains shopped there just to outfit their own ships for protection from pirates.

The coffeehouse was the busiest place in the city. Since most of a seaport's business was along the docks, so were the coffeehouses. Every day of the week, businessmen had "an ordinary" (a dinner) at two o'clock in the afternoon. Gentlemen could buy coffee, tea, chocolate, lemonade, wines, and liquors. In Philadelphia's coffeehouse, the customers could read the daily newspapers of large cities (of course some were weeks late) as well as the journals of the House of Assembly meeting at the State House. Business letters were addressed to men in care of the coffeehouse. The innkeeper also kept an alphabetical directory of all the principal tradesmen, merchants, brokers, and captains of vessels.

Eating to Order

"Having dinner out" was not the custom in 1787. Eating in public was a very unpleasant experience for many people. Cities had several taverns, but only a few restaurants. Philadelphia had Mr. Barry's chophouse, where men ate just what was put on the table, and Marinaud's French Restaurant, where ladies and gentlemen ate in the garden under a tent in summer. Winter or summer, however, Monsieur Marinaud had to be told the day before that guests were coming to dinner. There was no refrigerator or freezer, and his French pastry was "impossible to keep readymade."

The bakery was a very important shop to people who did not want to make their own bread every day. In Pittsburgh, the baker would not sell bread to anyone who did not give him either cash or flour. Frontier bakers like him were kept busy making biscuits to be packed in barrels for surveyors and travelers going down the Ohio River.

In Charleston, South Carolina, the bakers went on strike. A city law tried to make them stop adding sawdust and other powders to their flour. The bakers said they could not support their families if they had to use more flour in their bread. When they went on strike, the only bread that people could buy was ship bread, packed in barrels and hard as a rock. Angry people put this poem in the newspaper:

> BONE and SKIN, two bakers thin
> Would starve the town, or near it.
> But be it known to SKIN and BONE
> That Flesh and Blood won't bear it.

The confectionery shop was the place one went when planning a party. Some ready-made goodies were displayed in boxes—like sugar plumbs, nonpareils, lemon drops, cinnamon drops, peppermints, and barley sugars. The confectioner could make beautiful delicate flowers and figures out of sugar or thin shells from pastry. He made fine cakes, biscuits, macaroons, and "marchpanes" (marzipan). The confectioner made candied fruits that looked "just like nature." For travelers, he sold both lemon and punch syrup that needed only the addition of water. He rented table glasses decorated with sugar for special parties.

Since just about everyone dipped into the medical trade, the confectioner also had his candy that "never failed in coughs, asthmas, consumption and hectic fevers." He had marshmallow pastilles (tablets) for colds and "cashoo" (cashew) nuts to sweeten the breath. But his best-loved product was ice cream. There was no way to keep ice cream cold. Customers could buy it only "on previous warning." They told him a day ahead what time they would eat it and what kind they wanted.

Beware the Baths

As soon as Americans were used to "free enterprise," they began to think of new ways to make money. One Frenchman bought a house in Philadelphia and installed seven bathtubs made of sheet iron. This was long before anyone ever dreamed of having such a tub inside the home! Subscriptions to use the bathhouse cost $8 a month, or $1 for three baths. But Americans were suspicious of what might happen if they washed away the "protective coating" that nature put over their skins. Diseases might get inside through all those little pores in the skin.

Colonial Commercials

Advertising to persuade a customer to shop in a certain store was still new. Before the Revolution, certain shops had "royal approval" and they were the best shops. But now all shops were on the same footing. Shop owners were not sure whether they should beg customers to come to their shops or whether the customers should be teased in. They tried both.

Samuel House believed in the humble approach. He completed a lengthy list of the groceries he sold with this statement:

> He [Samuel House] is enabled to sell the above articles on such low terms as he flatters himself will give satisfaction to those who will be pleased to favor him with their commands which he humbly solicits.

But a seller of secondhand carriages thought that the American way of selling should have a little more humor, like this ad:

> TO BE SOLD:
> A chariot with new harness and two white horses
> A phaeton with ditto ditto and two brown ditto
> One ditto with ditto ditto and two black ditto
> One ditto with old ditto and without ditto
> Those inclined to purchase any of the above will please apply to the subscriber.

7

SIGHTS TO SEE IN THE NEW WORLD

In America, people don't ask What is He? but
What Can He Do?
    Benjamin Franklin, about 1790

The day was very quiet, thought James Flack, as his horse plodded through the deserted street of a little Connecticut town. The peaceful silence relaxed him a little from thoughts of the business trip and the long road ahead to Boston. Suddenly, a man with a very stern face stepped from the side of the road into the center and grabbed the reins.

Highwayman! The dreaded word raced into James's mind. He remembered uncomfortably that he had no gun or any way to defend himself. Then the man spoke sternly.

"Get down from your horse," he said. "And come to meeting. 'Tis the Lord's Day."

"No, thank you," said James, as politely as he could manage after the scare. "I have business in Boston and have no time to stop."

"Come to meeting," said the man angrily. "You will spend this day in our town."

"I will not," said James, getting angrier by the second. A crowd had gathered, and James appealed to them, but his words fell on deaf ears. A sheriff appeared, fined him for disturbing the peace on the Lord's Day, and hauled him off to jail. James spent the rest of the day and part of the next in jail writing a letter to a newspaper editor he knew. He wrote:

> Dear Mr. Printer,
> I brought my family to America where we hoped to live free from shackles of religious bigotry. Before this event, I sincerely thought that the person of the lowest citizen in America was as sacred as the person of any king in Europe and that his liberty in any sense could not be invaded without grossly violating the laws of the land. If I'm to be forced into a religious meeting, I might as well go home.

Travelers usually stayed away from New England and even some towns in New Jersey on a Sunday. But James Flack's angry letter was printed in newspapers in many cities and made other traveling people angry, too. Within a few years, those religious persons who had tried so hard to push travelers into their church pews were learning a new lesson. Freedom of religion meant that travelers who did not want to go to church had their rights, also.

Mud and Murder

No matter what day travelers chose for their trip, they could be sure of finding problems ahead. They could choose to go on horseback, by stage wagon, or by ship, but travel was not fun. Surprisingly, travelers did not complain often. Everyone lacked something when traveling, and ordinary lives were so filled with discomforts that a few more, during the enjoyment of a trip, did not matter much.

Mr. Anderson, his son Tommy, and their friend Mr. Gibbons decided one day on a short trip on horseback from Charleston, South Carolina, to a small town in Georgia. Today the trip might take two hours, with time out for a hamburger. But the three people in 1787 were happy to make it in six days. The road was often no more than a high narrow path with water on both sides.

"Crossing the canal dividing Mr. Ash's place from Mr. Glover's, my boy's horse fell in and with great difficulty, we got him out," said Anderson. "We were continually plung-

Tourists are glad to find a highway through a pass in the Allegheny Mountains

Pulpit Rocks was an oddity that made people
remember this was uncivilized country

ing into mud and water four feet and more deep. Mr. Gibbons' horse fell into a watercourse. I frequently found myself
standing on the mud—while I was straddling my horse!"

Young Tommy was small and lightweight, so he went
ahead to test bridges and roadways to see if they would hold
the weight of the two men. Once the three travelers had to
swim their horses across a swamp. While they were saddling
up again, Anderson's pistol dropped into the water, wetting
its load of powder. Later that day, as they were leading their
horses over some planks on a bridge, they were suddenly
surprised by a man walking toward them. As soon as their
horses were safely over the bridge, the man ran a short
distance and mounted a big horse that was being held for
him by another man. Then he stood silently in the center of
the road. Gibbons and Anderson urged their horses forward
very slowly. Anderson could think only about his pistol

loaded with wet gunpowder. There was no way for the three
to defend themselves from highwaymen. The man in the
road stubbornly stood his ground. The three decided it
would be safer to turn and recross the plank bridge. Much
later, they learned that the other man had been afraid *they*
were going to rob *him*.

Sea Voyage

The most comfortable way to see the sights of the united
states—after a few days of seasickness—was to take a coastal
ship. Sea passengers paid $8 to travel between Charleston
and Norfolk if they carried their own food. Those who ate
what the captain supplied paid $12. The trouble with sailing
was that the passengers never knew how long their trip
would take. A ship that sailed from Charleston to Norfolk
took three days, with the wind behind. But travelers going
the opposite direction had the wind in their faces, and the
same trip might take three weeks.

In France and England, many people asked Benjamin
Franklin what his country was like. Well-educated people
thought there must be jobs in the new world that no Americans would be qualified to fill and asked if they should apply.
Others had heard rumors that the new American government was so desperate for settlers that it was giving free
land and Negroes to work for people who came over. Franklin tried to set them straight.

"There is a common joke in America," Franklin told
them. "The white man makes the black man work, the horse
work, the ox work, and everything else work. Except the
hog. The hog is the only one in America who eats, drinks,

walks about and goes to sleep when he pleases. He lives like a gentleman."

The kind of people who should travel to America, Franklin told them, were those ready to work hard for a living. Very poor people in Europe could do much better in America where they might find work in some of the great new factories. People with very many children would find land for all their sons in the new world. The country needed carpenters and shoemakers. Young people who wanted to be apprentices would find a much better deal in America.

William Rollinson was just one of the thousands of people who sailed to the new world. Leaving his wife and baby in England until he could send for them, he paid $70 to sail on the *Nancy* in November of 1788. Winter crossings were the worst, but Rollinson was too seasick to notice that the captain immediately rationed everyone to two quarts of water a day. By February, the passengers were down to the last butt (barrel) of water and had to limit themselves to one quart a day until they landed in New York.

At last the captain ordered soundings to be taken, giving the passengers hope that land was near. Taking soundings meant letting down a 19-pound weight that had a hole in the bottom. Some grease from the galley had been put in the hole, and when the weight touched the bottom of the ocean, some of the sand stuck in the grease. Experienced mariners could tell exactly what part of the American coast they were near as soon as they saw the sample that came up clinging to the grease. When the soil was dumped on the deck, Rollinson put his toe over it and announced, "For the first time I have set my foot on American ground."

Haven at Last

On Friday, the thirteenth of February, the sea-weary passengers reached the entrance to New York harbor. But the wind was blowing out of the harbor so hard that no ships could go in. Sailing ships had to wait for the wind to come from the right direction. Next day, the ship was covered with two inches of ice. The passengers could see houses along the shore, but a smart gale still whipped out of the

Special sights to see in New York included the
Battery, the "Fly Market," and the prison

harbor. On the fifteenth, the ice around the ship's ropes was as thick as a man's body. The sailors had to keep chopping it off, without chopping the ropes by mistake, or the ship would become top-heavy and roll over. In the late afternoon the wind finally changed, and the *Nancy* passed the lighthouse at Sandy Hook. The next morning, the passengers landed in New York.

Travelers to the new world were the most excited about seeing the cities. Many were surprised to see that there really were cities after the many stories they had heard of the savage, undeveloped continent. New York was not the largest city, but its traffic was already so bad that soon some streets would be declared one-way only for traffic. The thunderings of coaches, chariots, chaises, wagons, and drays racing through the narrow, crooked streets was deafening to strangers. The city banned wagons with ironbound wheels in an effort to quiet the streets.

Visitors were fascinated by the horse-drawn carts that delivered "tea water" from a pump on Queen Street for a penny a bucket. New Yorkers told visitors that soon there would be aqueducts to carry water under the streets and lead pipes to carry the water straight into their homes. No one worried about sanitation. Pigs ran loose through the city, eating the garbage almost as soon as it was thrown into the streets. Farmers, who needed fertilizer for their farms, collected the manure that street cleaners piled up.

Tourists in New York headed for the famous sights. The law courts and prison, the "Fly Market" where the greatest varieties of fruits and vegetables could be found, and the old Sugar-House Prison where Lord Howe had kept American prisoners, were sights not to be missed. Two churches attracted attention. The steeple of St. Paul's Church made it

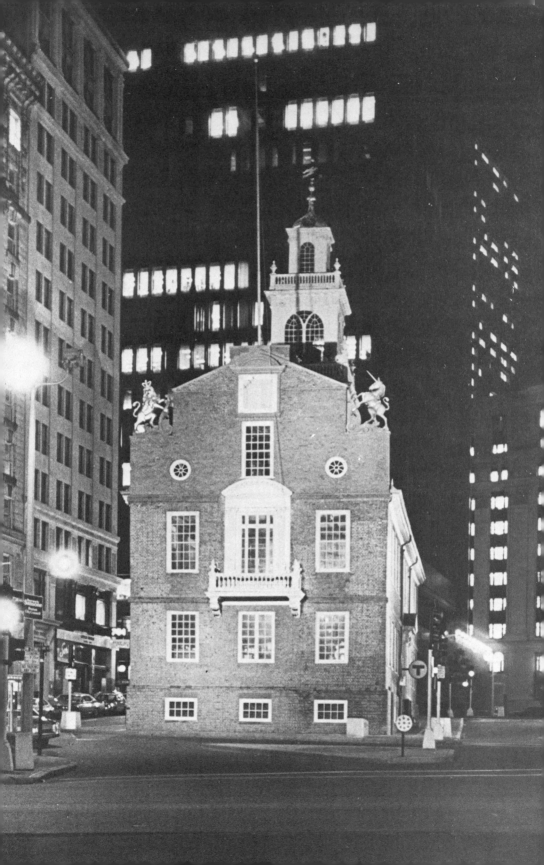

The State House in Boston looks now just as it
did to 1787 tourists. Only the neighborhood has
changed

the tallest building in the city and the steeple of the Old
Dutch Church was where Benjamin Franklin had experi-
mented with lightning. The fort at the Battery was another
sight, although most people felt that enemy ships could easily pass by the fort when there was a stiff breeze to fill their
sails. Even though it would not be much good as a fort,
people said, "it makes a nice breezy walking place for the
citizens, anyway."

The most important building in the city was only three
stories high. It was known as the City Hall until March 1789,
when it became known as Congress or Federal Hall. Inside,
the building was large and impressive, with a view clear to
the roof. Outside was the balcony where George Washington took the oath as the first President. Above the balcony
was the figure of a large eagle with a glory that appeared to
be bursting from a cloud.

North from New York, up the Post Road, was Boston.
Traveling through the countryside on the way to Boston,
strangers were most surprised to see the many stone fences
and the houses of wood. "Stones could be one of the riches
of this country," said one traveler, "if only they would build
houses of them." Passing through Rhode Island, people were
surprised to see so many lovely flower gardens. They had
heard that cultivated plants would never grow in the wild
soil of America.

When travelers arrived in Boston several days later, they were happy to learn that walking was no longer forbidden on Sundays. Bostoners now even enjoyed music and card-playing occasionally. Everyone went to see the first college in America. Harvard stood on a plain about four miles from the city in a village called Cambridge. Now that its president had decided to stop teaching only the dead languages, the college was growing fast. Other important sights to visit were the Almshouse for the poor people and the Workhouse where criminals were kept busy.

Unusual Sights

In 1786, the most "stupendous work of the kind in America" was open to the public—the bridge across the Charles River from Boston to Charles Town. The builders of this remarkable bridge became so famous that they were invited to sail to Ireland, with American lumber, and build another bridge there, just like it.

Sometimes visitors to Boston took a trip down to see Plymouth and Cape Cod. The soil on Cape Cod was so bad that the government had declared all the people who lived there to be free from taxes and gave them a bounty to carry on a fishing trade. An interesting island off the coast was Nantucket, where the whalers kept five whale-oil plants busy. Nantucket children went to school until they were twelve years old. Then, after two years of apprenticeship, they went to sea to learn whaling. The whalers along the docks talked about how far they had to sail now to find whales. Someday, they said, they might have to sail their ships as far as the Pacific Ocean for whales, but no one really believed they would have to travel far to find whales.

The largest city in the united states, Philadelphia, was already famous for having the largest building—the State House. Travelers from everywhere knew that was where the Declaration of Independence had been signed. Now in 1787, the convention was meeting there to write a new Constitution. Not every city could boast it had a town clock. The State House had two, one facing east and one west. In the same block, a new building was being erected for the first scientists in the country, the American Philosophical Society. Its members had offered prize money to the person with the best discovery or most useful invention in the fields of navigation, astronomy, or natural science.

Philadelphia had other notable sights to see. Prison reformers came from all over to see the city's jail in 1790—the first one to have individual cells for criminals. Medical men came to visit the first free clinic for poor people at Pennsylvania Hospital. The prettiest place to take a summer walk was through the gardens of the House of Correction. Then there was the Waterworks. At the edge of the Schuylkill River, an awe-inspiring pump which worked by waterpower carried the river water up the hill to a reservoir. From there, the water ran downhill through pipes into the houses of the city people.

Sights and Cities

Visitors who wanted to mix fun with their learning went to the only museum in the new world to see Charles Willson Peale's collection of oddities. In a special theater, tourists could view a thrilling panorama show of "Jerusalem" which made them feel they were standing in the ancient city. In the summer, people saw the first circus in the united states, owned by J. B. Ricketts.

South of Philadelphia was Baltimore, which had almost 2,000 houses, but it was built on a bay that was not deep enough for the largest ships. Only a few streets were paved, and the stagnant water there made the city unhealthy. Travelers thought Baltimore would probably never grow into a large city. They hurried on to the village of Alexandria, about sixty miles south, where there was a far greater parade of luxury. Servants wore silk stockings and boots and the women dressed elegantly, with feathered headdresses. During the war, while Alexandria was in the hands of the

The "Federal City" was swamps and forest in 1787. Even this view, seven years later, gives no hint of the Washington, D.C., we know

Americans, the British had tried to burn it. A ship carrying explosives was on the way up the Potomac River, but it ran aground and never reached the village.

Near Alexandria was the land that had been chosen for Federal City, the unbuilt capital of the united states. Very little could be said for the place. There were no roads of importance that led to it. The land was nothing but swamps and forest. In 1786, the united states had not even had the money to start building a city there. A man named Pierre L'Enfant seemed to think the site had great possibilities, however. He was planning to build a great National Pantheon to hold the bodies of the country's great heroes. Only one building had been finished by 1791, and it became a patent office instead of a Pantheon. A year later, the cornerstone was laid for what was to be the President's house. Many people thought Federal City should be named for General Washington.

Williamsburg, Virginia, was a pleasant enough city, but it was decaying now that the government of the state had moved to Richmond. Too much in Williamsburg reminded people of the English rule. Noah Webster remarked that its College of William and Mary and its public town clock and bell were its only assets.

The Inland Shift

North Carolina had some important towns that looked to people as though they would grow to be very large. Edenton, on the waters of Albemarle Sound, was an important seaport. The women of Edenton had thrown tea into the water in 1774, before the better-known Boston Tea Party took place. But Edenton never grew, because the government built the Dismal Swamp Canal. All the business that used to go to Edenton went to Elizabeth City, North Carolina, after 1790. The same thing happened to Bath Town, a seaport on Pamlico Sound where the first settlers had landed. Bath Town had been so important it almost became the capital of North Carolina, but now it was losing business. Instead, Washington City, named for General Washington, was becoming the shipping center.

Farther down the coast, Charleston, South Carolina, was a large and important seaport. But people had begun to move inland, away from the sea. Since the border of South Carolina seemed to go all the way to the Mississippi River, many people felt the capital should be moved. One group of people decided to start a town they would call Columbia. In 1786, the Charleston newspaper said the whole area for the new city was nothing but a "waste plain." This made the Columbia settlers stubborn. They sold lots on their "waste plain" for 25 pounds sterling and announced boldly that Columbia would someday be the state capital. One week after the lots went on sale, the settlers began digging the foundations for the state house, just to prove they meant it. The lots sold fast and before the year was out the state capital was moved there from Charleston.

Savannah, an important seaport in Georgia, had competition, too. The city of Sunbury was larger and had dozens of square riggers calling at its docks on the Medway River. A fort had protected the city during the Revolution and now it was used when there was trouble with the Indians. Sunbury had an academy that attracted both boys and girls from all over the south. The homes were built of "tabby" (a long-lasting combination of cement and seashells), with porches called "piazzas" to catch the summer breezes. The wharfs were made of palmetto pilings—the only kind of wood that the sea worms in southern waters would not eat away in a few months. Today all that remains of old Sunbury are the rebuilt fort and a road that leads to a boat-launching ramp.

Super River

Travelers had discovered that the united states had one "superhighway," called the Ohio River. Thousands of people were heading downstream. The *Pittsburgh Gazette,* the

Tourists passing through Virginia were amazed
at the already famous Natural Bridge

first newspaper west of the Allegheny Mountains, said this about the traffic:

> Between October 10, 1786 and December 1788, there has passed down the Ohio River 857 boats; 16,203 souls; 7,190 horses; 1,811 black cattle; 1,258 sheep; 563 wagons, and 1 phaeton. A number also passed in the night uncounted.

Pittsburgh people complained that their city was becoming "just a halfway-house—a resting place" for the people going downriver. They decided that their city was "the gateway to the west" and they could become rich by selling supplies to the flatboatmen before they left. In 1786, Pittsburgh had one minister, five lots for graveyards, a log church, two doctors (one of them British), two lawyers, and one high mound of buried Indians. The nearest courthouse was thirty miles away. Hogs ran loose in town, pushing open board fences, drinking from wells, and running through houses and gardens. But Pittsburgh had its newspaper, several retail stores, regular laid-out streets, and about a hundred houses of hewn logs with plastered inside walls.

Far downriver from Pittsburgh was one of the wonders of the new world—the new city of Marietta. In 1787 a group of New Englanders had built the first planned town in Indian territory. Two years later "the handsomest pile of buildings this side of the Allegheny Mountains" had been erected on top of the works of some ancient Indians. The fortifications were of hewn logs, with blockhouses two stories high built at each corner. On one of the blockhouses was a tower with a cupola and spire that held a bell—a symbol of civilization in the wilderness. The Marietta settlers proved that old world people were wrong when they said only wild things could be grown in the uncultivated soil. General Rufus Putnam said, "The beans, pumpkins, turnips, squash, cabbage, melons and cucumbers were the best I ever tasted."

"Kentucke" the Wonderful

Because Marietta was successful, many other settlers built towns in new places. Land in "Kentucke" was cheap, and an article in *New Jersey Magazine* in 1786 described it in such glowing terms that people flocked there to start more new villages. Kentucke, according to the magazine, was filled with wild plants to feed settlers—like black cherries, mulberries, honey locust to make beer, coffee trees which made good coffee, and pawpaws which tasted like cucumbers. The fish, fruit, and animals were plentiful enough to support thousands of settlers, and then there was the "buffola" which weighed up to 1,000 pounds and was covered with long, curly hair. Travelers to Kentucke went to see the white marble, the large caves, and a wagon road that had been "made by buffolas" at Leestown. The Kentucke country was still a part of the state of Virginia, until it became a separate state in 1786 and changed its name to Kentucky.

Americans discovered that there was no end to the unusual sights to find in their own land. Waterfalls, natural bridges, sinkholes, all shared honors with the large cities, navigable rivers teeming with fish, and the mountains that seemed unconquerable.

8

HARD TIMES

My life is done; my race is run
My resting place is here.
This stone is got to keep the spot
Lest men should dig too near.

Tombstone mentioned
in *The American Magazine*, 1787

"I received the smallpox by inoculation today," said
Nathan Webb on October 6, 1788. He was staying in Dr.
William Aspinwall's Hospital in Boston to wait for the
disease.

Smallpox killed eighteen out of a hundred people that
year. Most of Nathan's friends had ugly pockmarks all over
their bodies to show they had survived the disease and were
now immune to it forever. But until men, women, and children had had the disease, they never knew when it might
strike and end their lives.

Now modern medicine brought them choices. They could
wait for the smallpox to catch them. Then perhaps they
would die of it, because they were not in the best physical
condition when they became sick. Or they could catch it on

purpose, by having the doctor inoculate them at a time when they were feeling very healthy. Or they could take it "the natural way," by inoculating themselves during a visit to someone who had the disease. Doctors said it was best when they themselves inoculated a person, because then they could treat that person for three weeks before he or she broke out with the pox. Only one person in a hundred died after being inoculated by the physician.

"I led an idle life in the hospital," said Nathan. "No one was allowed to read on account of weak eyes. The diet was very simple . . . nothing but gruel, broth and bread. We slept on a straw bed at night."

For three weeks, Nathan and his roommate, Stephen Fox, had little to do but rest and talk. Another young man in the hospital with them was to be married as soon as he knew the smallpox was over. He spent all his time writing letters to his beloved. His letters were smoked before they left the hospital, but even though they were "sterilized," his girl's father would not let her read them for fear they carried the smallpox.

Bitter Medicine

The patients took antimony and mercury pills every day. Twice the doctor gave them "a puke." That was a bitter medicine that made them vomit everything inside. Another time, he gave them a "cathartic," which emptied them out the other direction. Then they were ready for the pox.

"I have about 400 of the pox," said Nathan happily. "About 60 of them are on my face." A great weight had been lifted from his mind. Now he was safe forever from the most dreaded disease of the century.

"I paid the doctor $8," he said, when it was safe to leave the hospital. "They washed and clensed my clothes when I left. And I received a Certificate that I was free from infection. The first thing I did was go to meeting [church], although my face looked rough after the 60 pustules on it."

Hundreds of people "took the smallpox in the natural way" that year, by visiting friends with the disease and inoculating themselves. Instead of going to the hospital as Nathan did, they lay in a closed-up room with a blanket over the door to keep out fresh air. Grown-ups wrapped the children's hands in rags to keep them from scratching the pox on their faces and making scars. Many of them died. The sad truth was that a real cure was on the way. Only a few years after Nathan's trip to the hospital, Dr. Edward Jenner of England discovered that milkmaids never seemed to get smallpox. They did get a harmless disease called "cowpox," though. In 1796, Jenner found that a vaccination with matter from a cowpox would not make a person sick and would free him forever from the smallpox.

"Doctors wear wigs so the size of their knowledge can be measured by the size of their heads," said one man. Actually there were two kinds of doctors—those who believed in bleeding people to make them better and those who believed in making them sweat. There were only a few medical schools in the united states and even in the schools a man (never a woman) became a doctor by paying a fee to follow the well-known doctors on their rounds through the hospital. In order to learn what was inside the human body, student doctors often stole the bodies of criminals from the graveyard and dissected them. But one day in April, 1788, the students dug up the body of a man of good reputation.

Real Doctors and Kitchen Doctors

On Sunday, a mob collected at the hospital in New York City. They destroyed all the anatomical preparations made for the students. The next day the rioters attacked the homes of many doctors, breaking their windows and smashing up their furniture. When some doctors fled to the local jail for protection, the mob turned on the jail. Armed with bricks and bats, they attacked the guards, who had muskets and swords. A few shots were fired and three of the mob lay dead. The next day, two cannons faced the rioters as they milled around Broadway. The ringleaders were taken to prison before the mob went home.

For medical advice, families turned first to mother. She had learned everything she knew from her mother and her grandmother's "receipts" in the cookbook. Nobody knew what to blame disease on. Doctors said it was "a breakdown in the life force from the brain" or perhaps "an imbalance of excitability in the body." Most people thought diseases came from smells, like the "pestilential vapors" from the garbage in the streets at night. They also wondered whether the people back in the old world had been right when they said the strange climate on this side of the ocean would make them sick.

The kitchen doctor was usually at her best with uncomplicated sicknesses. Sally Emerson rubbed her children's faces with sage to cure the "sun-burnt smart." To keep her children from getting rickets or to treat their sore eyes, she washed their heads every day with cold water. When her children had sores, she rubbed on turpentine. When the tiny "no-see-'em" bugs bit her children, she rubbed on the juice of radishes. In between times, Sally chased after flies in the house, sprinkling Spanish tobacco over their heads to kill them.

Tooth Carpenters

There were very few dentists for the children when they had toothaches. There were no dental schools and no books for dentists. Their main job was to pull out teeth that hurt, and they didn't always do that job well.

"I had two teeth extracted," said Noah Webster one September day. "One by mistake. This is hard indeed."

Parents did not allow their children to use a toothbrush more than three times a week because they thought brushing would make the teeth look long and deformed. Children had many toothaches because their teeth rotted. When a tooth hurt, mother softened some beeswax and stuffed it into the hurting place. When the ache grew worse and the whole side of the face hurt, the doctor came and gave a "blister" behind the ear. This was to "draw out the pain." Actually, it hurt so much that often the first pain was forgotten. If a pain continued for many days, the tooth was pulled out. No one realized that good teeth came from eating healthful food. Black people, and especially young black children, had constant toothaches. Doctors said that was because they ate their corn bread while it was still hot.

Dentists were called "tooth carpenters" for a good reason —they made false teeth for poor people out of wood. Ivory false teeth cost more money. George Washington hired a New York dentist, Dr. John Greenwood, to make him a

complete new set of false teeth. Greenwood was very clever
—he had invented a tooth drill that ran when he put his foot
on a treadle, like a spinning wheel. He made the base for
Washington's teeth from a hippopotamus tusk and screwed
human teeth into it.

One dentist, Dr. LeMayeur, said false teeth were not necessary. He transplanted human teeth right into his patients'
gums. The transplanted teeth stayed in place for a while—
and so did Dr. LeMayeur. Then, when the teeth began fall-
ing out and the patients complained of pain and swollen
gums, Dr. LeMayeur left town. Many people died from in-
fections after having teeth transplanted, but Dr. LeMayeur
had left town long before that. In 1783, he was living and
working in New York. In 1785, he was doing the same job
in Philadelphia. But now it was 1787 and the good doctor
had moved on to Charleston, putting this advertisement in
the local newspaper:

> Dr. LeMayeur, just arrived from the Northward, who has
> cured some thousands of the curry [did he mean caries?]
> upon the continent and has transplanted a great many teeth,
> may be spoke with at his lodgings at Mrs. Ramage's at No.6
> Cumberland Street. Any person, white or black (slaves ex-
> cepted) willing to part with any of their front teeth, shall
> receive 2 guineas [about $4] each.

No one ever thought of Dr. LeMayeur as a con artist.

The Criminal Type

"You need only look on the faces of the prisoners to lead
an honest life," said one traveler who had dropped into the
prison of a strange city, much as people today would go to

see the zoo. Several of the criminals were condemned to "work at the wheelbarrow." Chained to their wheelbarrows, they had to carry heavy rocks from one place to another all day. By 1788, some prisons decided the wheelbarrow made men worse instead of better.

Horse stealing was a serious crime and made people so angry that they organized groups of townspeople to give chase across the state if necessary. The horse thief who was caught by the group was lucky to escape with his life. But when he was taken to jail, he was given a ride on the wooden horse. Andrew Peters of Hartford had been caught and punished once before. When he was mounted on a wooden horse, his hands tied behind him, the sheriff wondered why he wasn't yelling when the horse was bounced up and down roughly. He discovered that Peters had stuffed a blanket into his pants, so Peters was invited to take another ride without the blanket.

The Hardest Life

Vandalism was a problem in cities. Many public lamps were broken, their glass lampshades smashed and the cups filled with oil stolen. Benjamin Franklin tried to design unbreakable streetlights for Philadelphia, but the vandals always found a way to destroy them. A vandal was fined 5 pounds the first time and 10 pounds the second time he was caught. In addition, he paid 25 pounds for each lamp broken. But the punishment was different for mulattoes or Negro slaves. They received 21 lashes at the public whipping post and were kept on bread, water, and hard labor for three days in the public workhouse. Only if a slave's master or mistress paid a large fine could he escape this punishment.

Every newspaper had its list of runaway apprentices. Learning how to do a job by becoming an apprentice for several years was not a bad system. The problem was that sometimes masters were cruel and apprentices ran from them. More often, apprentices ran away because they were young people and were impatient to get started in their own businesses without waiting to finish out their terms. But since apprentices were under contract to work for a certain number of years, it was illegal to run away.

Some of them had been apprenticed when they were no more than babies, like little Ned Fifer whose mother took him to Mrs. Drinker's house one day and left him.

"His mother wants to bind him to us until he's sixteen," said Mrs. Drinker, who already had a houseful of her own children. "He is now between eight and nine. I told her we would take him upon trial."

But little Ned was too young for the "busy-ness" of the Drinker household, and Mrs. Drinker sent him home to his mother. Mrs. Drinker had no husband and she could not afford to support him. Little Ned was bound out to another family.

Apprenticed children were not so badly off as handicapped children. People were superstitious about babies born with handicaps. Either the mother must have looked at someone crippled while she was carrying the child or else God was punishing one of the parents for some "secret" sin. They could think of no other reason for handicapped children. Often, when a mother had a badly deformed baby, she was told it had died at birth and the baby was taken away.

"I saw an object of charity today," said Noah Webster.

Even the writer of the dictionary had no better word for a handicapped person. "He was a cripple born in Dartmouth, Massachusetts, and was carried from his native place in youth. He lost his residence there because there was no record of his birth."

The crippled man Noah saw was then forty years old. His legs had never grown, and his arms, except for one hand, were useless. But he was in good health and mentally bright. He managed the horse that pulled his little cart by means of a rope he held in his one good hand. He had never known his parents and had no privileges of a citizen because the record of his birth had been destroyed. He earned his living by begging.

Every town had its Overseers of the Poor, who made a list of all the "deserving" poor who had no family to help them. Many on the list were wives and mothers whose husbands had been away longer than a year. They may have been dead, like Nancy Woodend's husband, who was killed by Indians on the Natchez Trace that year, or they may have deserted their families. A woman could return to the town where she had been born, if she could get there, and be cared for by the Overseers of the Poor.

Fire! Fire!

Of all the hard times that hit families, fire came the most often. As soon as a person heard the shout "Fire!" he or she (this was a job for women, too) grabbed a bucket and ran with the others. Each home had its leather fire buckets, marked with the owner's name so they could be returned. Any stranger who needed a bucket was free to go into the

The powerful pumping engine had solid wooden wheels that would not go around corners. But with two men pumping, it squirted water about 75 feet

entryway of any house and take the buckets with him to the fire.

When people arrived at the burning house, they formed a double line to the source of water. Women and young people stood in the empty-bucket line, helping to pass the buckets down to the water. The men stood in the other line, passing the filled buckets as fast as they could without spilling too much. The buckets of water were poured into the modern "pumping engine." The firemen, pumping the engine as fast as their arms would work, forced the water through a hose. With this modern machine, the water sometimes reached as high as the second floor of a house.

"I admire the Charleston police," said Timothy Ford. "They are not only provided with engines and the people taught to throw themselves into lines immediately upon their assembling for the purpose of conducting water, but every warden (of whom there are 13) is obliged to keep five hogsheads, strongly made and painted, full of water. On the first alarm, these are immediately to be rolled out of place to supply the engines until the lines can be formed. By this means, 65 hogsheads of water may reach the place of fire as soon as the engines themselves. They are then prevented from the delay and loss of time in the confusion of the people getting into order. This instant supply may sometimes check or extinguish a fire in its early stages which might otherwise make great headway."

Fires had a good head start anyway. The houses were covered with paint and their roofs were tarred shingles, the best of food for flames. A French visitor to the united states said, "There are so many willing helpers that there is little order and they do more harm than good." After the fire was over, there was the matter of celebrating the victory. The workers left the buckets in the streets and hoodlums played with them. Townspeople often had to search for their own buckets to take them home again.

Insurance companies charged much higher rates to people who had trees around their homes. When an insured house was on fire, people from the insurance company came to the fire to cheer on the bucket passers to work harder and faster. People who lived in the country or on the frontier did not have the comfort of buying insurance and had no mod-

Fires could rage out of control quickly, but this one had help. Patriots started it a few days after the British occupied New York, then slashed the hoses and took the bolts out of the machinery. Soldiers are trying to force men to fight the fire

ern pumping engines. Their only hope of stopping a fire was to throw buckets of water directly on the flames.

Frontier Fears

Cities built on the frontier had another danger besides fire —one that most older cities did not have. Only the Indians could have told new settlers what would happen when the ice upstream melted suddenly and sent a great freshet down the Muskingum River and flooded the town of Marietta. This had been Indian territory and the Indians watched silently as the waters crept higher.

"We got up at sunrise this morning," said young Thomas Wallcut on a cold February day. "The doctor calling and telling us the water rose so fast that it would soon be in the house, when I immediately got up. Before we could get our breakfast done, the water came in so fast that the floor was afloat and we stood in water to our buckles to drink the last dish of coffee." (Shoe buckles, that is; not belt buckles.)

Hard times along the frontier sometimes involved trouble with the Indians. Reports of massacres appeared in the newspapers along with other stories that told of Indian friendliness. Most Indian chiefs still hoped that the long conversations they held with the soldiers of the "thirteen council fires" would bring peace and some satisfactory way to divide the land. Ebenezer Denny, a young lieutenant, was not sure the soldiers were handling the ceremonies in the best way when a large body of Shawnees came to make a treaty.

"The Shawnees saluted us with three rounds per man," he reported. "So we had to give them the same honors because they are a very proud nation. Twelve men, under my command, were ordered to parade with three rounds of cartridges. We awaited their approach. They were very solemn. As they came up, they gave us Indian music beat on a keg drum by one of the chiefs, all singing at the same time. When their firing was over, I commenced and in the interval gave them a tune on drum and fife. Then I believe what we did was very degrading to the united states. A party of our soldiers cooked and served out provisions to them in the council house. With the Indians, the six most decrepit old women are used for that purpose. When they saw our soldiers carrying kettles of food, they laughed and called out, 'There come the old women with warriors' coats on!' Who knows but what they conceived us all as old women clad in uniforms."

Meanwhile, away from the frontier in more civilized

country, young men often killed each other in quarrels over
a lady or over imagined insults. Duels were more common
in the old country, where people lived close together and it
was easy for men to step on each other's egos. A man learned
to fight with a sword there. But in America, when a man had
to "defend his honor," it was done with fists or pistols.

"The lower class of people in America grow their finger-
nails long so they can scratch each other's eyes out," ex-
plained a Virginia man. "Gentlemen fight with pistols."

Burying the Dead

Young children often died in those days. The parents of
little Martha Laurens, age one, were crying when the doctor
told them their tiny girl had died of the smallpox. They
carried her out of the closed-up room in which she had lain
for days and set her in front of an open window to dress her
for her funeral.

The doctor walked past the baby and gasped, "She's
alive!"

Little Martha lived to be an old lady, with eleven children
of her own. But her father never got over the fright that he
might have buried his child while she was still alive. When
he died in 1792, he wrote in his will that his son could not
inherit his money unless he agreed to cremate his father.
Mr. Laurens' cremation was the first in the united states.

As soon as a person died, a horseback rider was sent to
round up for the funeral all the relatives and friends who
lived within a few days' journey. Not to attend a funeral
after being invited was unforgivable. The guests quickly put
on their dark funeral clothes, hitched up their wagons, and

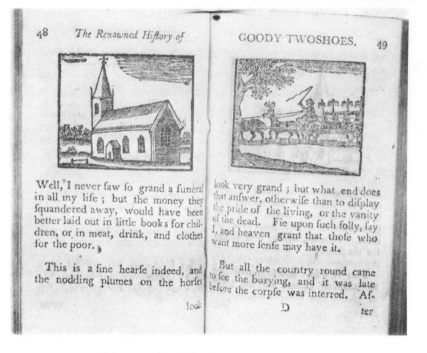

48 *The Renowned History of* GOODY TWOSHOES. 49

Well, I never faw fo grand a funeral in all my life ; but the money they fquandered away, would have been better laid out in little books for children, or in meat, drink, and clothes for the poor.

This is a fine hearfe indeed, and the nodding plumes on the horfes

look

look very grand ; but what end does that anfwer, otherwife than to difplay the pride of the living, or the vanity of the dead. Fie upon fuch folly, fay I, and heaven grant that thofe who want more fenfe may have it.

But all the country round came to fee the burying, and it was late before the corpfe was interred. Af-

D ter

A children's book describes a funeral, complete
with a fine hearse

headed toward the funeral place. The closest relations and friends, even children if the dead person was a child, served as pallbearers, carrying the coffin. Each pallbearer received a pair of gloves to keep as a remembrance.

The funeral services were held in the front parlor of the home. The minister came to the house and gave a suitable sermon. Then everyone, including the doctor, who walked beside the minister, walked to the cemetery, two by two. The coffin was carried on the shoulders of four bearers, while four more walked behind, ready to change places with them when they were tired. A married person's procession was headed by married couples walking in pairs. A child's funeral was led by children—a boy leading if a boy had died and a girl leading a girl's procession.

Coffins were made of every kind of wood. A simple one of pine was cheap, but a cedar coffin with the person's name carved on it cost 14 pounds (about $56). In the city, where cemeteries were crowded, several persons were buried in the same grave, one on top of another. At the end of the funeral, a slate stone marked with the name and dates of the dead person was put up at the grave. Travelers often went to visit cemeteries in a strange town, just as they went to see the waterworks or the prison. In 1791, one tourist who had always wanted to meet Benjamin Franklin at last did.

"I went into what is called the church burying ground and viewed the little spot that contains the earthly remains of Benjamin Franklin, once so popular and noted in his day amongst the Great and the Learned," said the tourist. "Death has now brought him on a level with the meanest."

On his grave, which can still be seen in Philadelphia, was this epitaph, which Franklin himself had written:

The Body
of
Benjamin Franklin, Printer

Like the cover of an old book
Its contents torn out
And stript of its lettering and gilding
Lies here, food for worms.
But the work shall not be lost
For it will appear once more
In a new and more elegant edition
Revised and corrected
By the Author.

Died 17 April 1790

Worse than Death

The only thing worse than death in the new country was slavery. Northern people who read the newspapers thought there were hardly any slaves left in 1788. Several papers reported that 10,000 black people had been returned from South Carolina and Virginia to a settlement in Africa near the mouth of the river Goree.

"Very few blacks remain in this country now," said the paper. "And we sincerely hope that in a few years every vestige of the infamous traffic in the human species, carried on by our ancestors, will be done away."

Many people living in both the north and the south were disgusted with slavery. They still remembered reading about the trial of a ship captain only a few years before. The captain had been told there was not enough drinking water on the ship for his crew and his cargo of slaves. So he had ordered 132 slaves to be thrown overboard while they were still handcuffed. Some slaves whose hands were free jumped after them. When the ship arrived in Jamaica a few days later, there were still 420 gallons of water left. The subscribers who had hired the captain to transport the slaves wanted to be paid for the lost slaves. The trial was not to punish the captain for murdering the slaves, but to make him pay for them. When the first mate testified that he had thrown the slaves overboard on his captain's orders without even considering whether it was a criminal act, everyone in the courtroom shuddered. The captain was found not guilty.

Many states now had laws against holding slaves. In New Jersey, masters had to teach their slaves to read. No slaves were allowed in the new Northwest Territories. But just because slaves could not be held in certain states does not mean there were no slaves there. There were many ways of getting around laws. An advertisement in the *Pennsylvania Packet* shows one way to avoid a law:

> Negro woman 22 years of age to be sold. Must be sold out of state as law will not admit of her being sold in it. Can cook. Has had smallpox. Fit for any kind of housework. Or will exchange for smart likely negro boy or girl about 15 years of age who is registered agreeable to laws in this state.

Many Negroes took the chance to run for freedom when they arrived in "free" states. Glasgow, age twenty, belonged to Captain Hirst of the schooner *Whim*. When the *Whim* docked in Philadelphia, Glasgow started running. His master offered a $10 reward for him and described him as "very black and smooth face [this meant he had not had smallpox] with large eyes that show much white. He will try to pass for a free man . . . is stout [meaning strong, not fat], well-made, sensible, rude and bold looking, wearing a green cloth coat, white breeches, stockings, has remarkable large feet, fond of gambling and a cheating rascal . . . born near Dover, Delaware . . . his mother belongs to Mr. William Carpenter of Delaware."

If Glasgow ran toward the Quaker meeting house or toward the Society for Promotion of Manumission of Slaves in Philadelphia, there is a good chance he made it to freedom. But even as a free black, his life would not have been ideal. There was always the chance that he or his family could be kidnapped and sold back into slavery.

Running to Freedom

A free black could get into slavery by mistake, like Judith Cocks who traveled from New England (where she knew practically nothing about slavery) to live in the south for a while with Mrs. Woodbridge. She took with her her little son, Jupiter. Judith had lived in the south only a short time, when she became ill and wanted to go back to New England. Since she was "free," Mrs. Woodbridge gave her permission to return to her former home. But Jupiter was just a little boy. Judith was told he would have to stay until he was twenty-five years old. Judith wrote a letter back to James Hillhouse in New England for help.

> My little son Jupiter is my greatest care. From the useage he meets with, I am all most distracted. He has to stay till he's 25 years of age . . . I thought he was to return with me to New England. I had much rather he would return and live with you as she [Mrs. Woodbridge] allows all her sons to thump and beat him the same as if he were a Dog.

Every newspaper had descriptions of slave runaways. Masters advertised in newspapers to the north with tempting offers of rewards. The description was always thorough, like this one of four blacks who escaped from John Edmonds' plantation at Berry's Ferry, Virginia.

> Toney, about 35, height 5'9", well-made, very artful and speaks slow, has a remarkable way of gritting his jaw teeth when spoke to. Has scar on right breast below his collarbone 4–5" long, the flesh higher than other part, occasioned by tree falling on him.
>   Bob, same height, round-made and well proportioned, very black with small eyes which generally appear red or yellow-

ish, speaks loud and bold with much confidence, about 25 years old.

Jeffrey, same height, age, but rather spare made and not so strait nor altogether so black as the others. His ankle bones very much in and under his feet with very narrow heels which leaves a print on the ground very broad where the hollow of his foot should be. Also several warts or lumps on his nose, slow speech and deceitful look.

Pleasant, a very low woman, wife to Toney, but well set, large features. Has lost all or greater part of her foreteeth. Walks briskly and lively and at times very complaisant. She has lately gave suck as she left a young child behind about 8 or 9 months old. She is much the complexion of Jeffrey, about 25 years of age. Took with her sundry clothes such as country cloth habits, striped in the warp. The others took with them their negro cotton jackets and long breeches made of negro cotton, osnaberg shirts, such as negroes generally wear in Virginia.

Toney is a tolerable carpenter. He and Bob saw well at the whipsaw. Reward 5 pounds each, if out of state. 3 pounds, if in the state.

During these years after the Revolution, slaves came as close to being freed as they would for the next seventy-five years. Preachers going through the south had convinced many plantation owners that their slaves should be freed. Many were set free on the spot. Other owners stated in their wills that certain slaves (and sometimes even their children) should be freed after the master's death. James, a slave of William Armistead, was freed by the state of Virginia because he had served as a spy during the Revolution. But for most black people, if the chance for freedom did not come before 1792, it would not come again before their great-great-grandchildren were born.

The southern plantations were mostly tobacco fields. The owner did not need a large number of slaves to grow tobacco. But as soon as the cotton gin made cotton a valuable crop to grow, plantation owners needed hundreds more slaves to help in their fields. The work was extremely hard, the hours long, and the conditions terrible. What were already hard times for slaves soon became intolerable times.

9

SPECIAL DAYS

No more days than 30 hath the month of
    September
The same may be said of June, April, Novem-
    ber.
The rest of the months are just 30 and 1
Except that short month February alone,
Which to itself claimeth just 8 and a score
But in every leap year, we give it one more.
    From *The Schoolmaster's Assistant,* 1784

"On Tuesday evening, we went to Mr. Outiens' ball in Danvers," said Catherine Saunders when her brother Charles came home from college. "I really think the Danvers people have taken up the business of dissipation, for there is another ball this week."

Balls were new and exciting to Catherine and her sister, Martha. But the terror of not being able to attract a man to ask them to dance almost spoiled the fun.

"As you may suppose," Catherine went on, "we cast our eyes eagerly round in search of someone to ask us to dance. But our spirits were not revived by the survey. There was

Mr. Samuels. But he was devoted, and rightly so, to Miss Osgood. We looked at Mr. William Gray—but we did not dare hope he would ask us. There were only two men we could reasonably hope to dance with . . . and they were quite old."

Catherine and Martha, chatting and smiling nervously from behind their fans, had seated themselves on "the handsome wing," the bench at the edge of the dance floor.

"Our eyes were bent toward the door—when in came two men. The whispers started by their arrival had just stopped when more whispers started at the entrance of George Goodman."

Catherine would not have missed this ball for anything. But she was in agony. She hoped her smile did not look desperate.

"Suddenly, our fortunes took a favorable turn. Mr. William Gray stepped up and paid us his compliments. Soon after, he escorted Mr. Goodman and Mr. Collins to the handsome wing. You can imagine our happiness."

Peaceful Revels

There were all kinds of balls in the united states, now that there was peace to celebrate. Balls ranged from the very snobbish kind—the kind to which a shop owner or a person in trade would never be invited—to "forest balls" given by country people who never dreamed of silk ball gowns. The women wore homespun dresses. The men paid the fiddler 7 shillings to play all night, and everybody drank ginger cider. Well into the morning hours, country people danced the Soldier's Joy, Innocent Maid, Rural Felicity, Soldiers

Gay, Sirrah, and the Virginia reel Fire in the Mountains, Run, Boys, Run.

When there were no balls in a town, there was always dancing school. Hundreds of young French gentlemen had come to America while a revolution brewed at home. They had no skills. They could not build, shoe horses, plow, or raise wheat. They had spent their lives going to balls, and dancing was what they did best. So they started dancing schools at the very moment that Americans discovered they liked to dance.

People of all ages flocked to dancing schools to learn contra dances, the minuet, and German dances. The dances performed by French royalty had a peculiar appeal to Americans, who no longer had any royalty of their own. Each French dancing master tried to make his own school sound the best.

Monsieur Sicard, for example, claimed to be a pupil of the assistant master of the first dancer of the Paris Opera, who had taught Marie Antoinette to dance. Most of his students did not get that all straight, but instead told their friends that he was Marie Antoinette's teacher. He taught ladies from ten o'clock in the morning until one in the afternoon, three days a week. From six to nine in the evening, he taught the gentlemen at $1 a lesson. But his biggest inducement was his machines—"the same machines used for the pupils of the Opera in Paris to turn at the same time the toes, knees and hips, by which means many inconveniences are prevented and ladies and gentlemen much eased in their gait."

Birthdays were always special occasions. George Washington's, on February 22, was a big day—even in 1789. Benjamin Franklin celebrated his eighty-first year at the Bunch of Grapes Tavern in Philadelphia. As usual, the partygoers pro-

Benjamin Franklin's home, printshop, and post
office as it looked in 1787

posed toasts to everything from "the liberty of the press" to
"the typesetters." Americans were soon to drop this custom
of drinking toasts. It was just another custom that was not
"American."

Most older people used their birthdays to take a look at
their lives. People did not expect to live long. They believed
their bodies changed very much every seven years. From
age twenty-one, life was all downhill.

Young people loved to visit friends and relatives. Because
travel was so hard, visits lasted days and sometimes weeks.

Lucinda Lee's special days came when she visited her cousin Nancy in Virginia. Like most girls of fifteen, they spent a great deal of time giggling and eating. For brief moments, they tried to improve their minds by reading good books. But always there were more interesting things to do.

"We had a great frolic one night," said Lucinda, "by eating in bed. We had a big dish of bacon and beaf, followed by a bowl of sago cream and after that an apple pye."

The girls had just taken off their wrappers (bathrobes) and were thinking about going to sleep, when Nancy said she was still hungry.

"We took it in our heads to want oysters," Lucy reported. "So we got up, put on our rappers and went down in the Seller to get them. Do you think Mr. Washington [an older cousin] did not follow us and scear us just to death? We went up though and eat our oysters anyway."

Sometimes a special day meant working and playing at the same time. Men had logrollings, barn raisings, and stump-clearing bees in the country. The women cooked the food and became the men's partners at the family "kick-up" that followed the work. Women had quilting bees, spinning bees, and candy frolics where boys and girls got all tangled up pulling taffy. A "changework" day was when several men joined together to do large jobs. "Changework" began with one man saying, "I'll help you pull out your stumps if you'll help me plow my field." When a large group of women got together to clean one house, they called it a "whang."

Folks who liked bargains never missed a vendue. These special auction sales were advertised ahead to draw a crowd. The person having the vendue put signs on trees and at the tavern so everyone would know what day to come. The guests sat on benches and passed around the articles to be

sold. George Nelson bought a pair of single-temple spectacles for 18 cents and discovered he could read small print
with them. Thomas Wallcut went to a vendue in Ohio and
found something he had been wanting a long time.

"At Mr. Parson's vendue I bought two pounds of coffee, so
that we are now like to have coffee for a change, I hope. Tea
has been our diet night and morning ever since I come to
Ohio except twice."

Holiday Habits

Special days that came once a year included St. Patrick's
Day, even though there were not a great many Roman
Catholics in the united states yet. The Irish were a minority,
and a great many jokes made fun of the Irish people. The
Irish Catholics who were in the country were very unhappy
at the way St. Patrick's Day was celebrated by the Protes-
tants. Some still "burned the Pope" and St. Patrick with
bonfires, until a Quaker in Philadelphia remarked, "The
people don't forget St. Patrick's Day, as it is called. They still
make a mock of the poor Irish saint. But if he is in Heaven,
it can't do him any harm."

May Day was celebrated with the first picnic of the year.
Men put a sprig of green in their hats or a tuft of deer's tail.
Sailors fastened green branches to the ends of their ships'
yardarms. There was always a parade, although few men
had uniforms, as brothers-in-arms got together for a sort of
Veterans Day. After the parade, everyone enjoyed a barbe-
cue with oxen roasted whole over huge fires. Grandparents
gave toys to little ones.

"Aerostaticks" had become an exciting part of Fourth of

July festivities, but since the big balloons often exploded in the air, people seldom went up in them. One boy of thirteen who did was Edward Warren. Edward, the first aeronaut in the united states, went up in Peter Carnes's balloon in Baltimore on June 23, 1784. Shortly after, Carnes tried to go up himself, and his balloon burst into flames. Philadelphians saw their first successful balloon ride on January 9, 1793, when François Blanchard took off from the jailhouse courtyard. President Washington gave him a presidential order to carry. After 46 minutes in the air, Blanchard landed unharmed in Gloucester, New Jersey.

Christmas was primarily a religious holiday. No presents to be opened on Christmas morning, no Christmas tree, no Santa Claus, no carols. No matter what day of the week Christmas fell on, the church service was the big event of the day.

"The galleries, aisles and pews were all full," said Nathan Webb one Christmas afternoon. "The broad aisle was so full that the sexton could not light the candles. So the people sitting under the candlesticks had to lift up a man on their shoulders who lit the candles instead. This naturally caused some mirth, even though it was indecent on such an occasion. Although there were some instruments, only the organ could be heard. Mr. Ray sang Handel's *Messiah.*"

In the evening on Christmas, there were parties.

"We had a dance with twelve ladies and five gentlemen," said Webb. "There were nuts and raisins for the ladies. For supper we had punch, cold roast beef and fowl. Nothing out of pocket," he added, glad for the chance to save some money.

Perhaps he was saving it for New Year's Day, the time that people exchanged small gifts. In Boston, the church bells rang the whole night through. But in Philadelphia it was the custom for anyone with a gun to "fire out the old year." On the New Year's Eve before 1787 began, William Morris' barn was set on fire by guns. Ten tons of hay inside fueled the fire so violently that his house almost burned down, too. Angry Philadelphians decided that if the police would not stop this dangerous and annoying custom, they would patrol the streets and roads themselves.

New Year's Day was a time of feasting. Dining rooms were set up, with the food displayed on one table for people to see. But they did not serve themselves. They sat at another table to be served the dishes they had seen. Around the soup bowl which was in the center were platters holding cod's head, roast beef, scotch collops (veal), leg of lamb, plum pudding, petit patties, boiled chicken, and tongue. After people had eaten the first course, the second was set out in the same way. In the center were jams and jellies and around those were roast turkey, woodcocks, marinated smelts, leg of lamb (the same one that was there in the first course), almond cheese cakes, minced pies, larks, and lobsters.

Special Celebrations

But these were just annual special days. Some special days would come only once in a lifetime, and Americans celebrated them with noise, pomp, and food.

April 19, 1783—eight years after Paul Revere's famous ride—was the first of these special occasions. The British had not even left New York yet. American and British soldiers were ordered to stand, although they were in their own separate camps, to listen to the words being read to them:

"The Commander in Chief orders the cessation of hostilities to be declared . . ."

In every American city, the people were reading the words or hearing them read aloud. Peace had come at last. The soldiers would soon hang their muskets over their own fireplaces and start plowing their land. Prisoners of war would be coming home. Within a week, ten thousand Americans who had been Loyalists would leave for Nova Scotia. Gunpowder had been turned into fireworks which were on sale to celebrate the peace.

Listening to the reading of the peace treaty, people joked about the taxes that would never touch them now. "In England," they said, "people are taxed in the morning for the soap that washes their hands. At nine, for their coffee, tea, and sugar. At noon for the starch that powders their hair. At dinner for the salt that savors their meat. In the evening, for the wine that cheers their spirits. All day long for the light that enters their windows and at night for the candle that lights them to bed." Before many years, Americans too would be paying many taxes, but right now it was time to celebrate.

Huge parades and illuminated houses, lit with every candle that could be spared, made the cities bright. Everywhere was the number thirteen—thirteen cannons firing thirteen rounds, thirteen platoons firing their muskets thirteen times, thirteen toasts proposed and drunk.

A few weeks later, a group of soldiers met in New York to form the first veterans group. The soldiers named it the Society of the Cincinnati, after a Roman general who had left his farm to lead the Romans into battle. A descendant of one of these Society of the Cincinnati soldiers found himself on both sides of the Revolution. He was Winston Churchill.

Pageantry Gone Awry

The following January, after the Treaty of Peace had been ratified by Congress, one very special day in Philadelphia fizzled. After months of work, a gigantic arch was finished on Market Street. The Pennsylvania Assembly had paid 600 pounds for the most impressive "demonstration of joy" that artist Charles Willson Peale could raise. Peale's Triumphal Arch rose forty feet high and was topped with a statue of Peace. Beautiful oil paintings decorated all of the arch. They were to be lighted by 1,150 lamps. Inside the arch were ladders and platforms for the men who were to launch 700 skyrockets as soon as a signal was given.

On January 22, the Triumphal Arch was to blaze into glory such as no American had ever seen. The crowd waited for the last lamp to be lit and for the musket shot that was to signal the start of the fireworks. Suddenly, one renegade rocket shot off too soon.

It struck the Arch, which was built of paper, canvas, and flammable oil paints; the whole Arch quickly burst into flames. Inside, precariously balanced on ladders and platforms, was the builder, Peale. He leaped down, into a stack of exploding rockets, and bounced farther down onto a platform, breaking his ribs. The rockets took off in every direction.

"The oiled pictures took fire and immediately communicated to the powder," said Elizabeth Drinker, who was

The State House in Philadelphia as it looked in 1778

standing in the crowd. "It blew up the whole affair, so as entirely to spoil the sport. Several lives [actually, only one] were lost by the sudden going off of the rockets."

The suspense that came before the grandest Fourth of July of them all began building slowly. First there had been that flop of a convention in Annapolis. Then, one after another, the states had chosen delegates to go to another convention in Philadelphia, and the writing of a new Constitution had begun. At long last, in October, the completed Constitution had appeared in the newspapers of every city.

Now, if only the states would ratify it! Tension built up as, one at a time, the separate states agreed to accept it. Delaware . . . then Pennsylvania . . . then New Jersey. The smallest state of all, Rhode Island, had not even sent a delegate. Would Rhode Island try to talk the other states out of joining the union? By the end of May, eight of the states had accepted it. Only one more was needed. Then, less than two weeks before July 4, 1788, two more states ratified! Naturally, people went wild celebrating The Fourth.

The Fourth of July

In Pittsburgh, joyous Americans gave three cheers and threw their hats in the air. They had already prepared thirteen piles of wood, one for each state. Nine of the piles were lighted and burned brightly. Green leaves and heavy boughs were thrown on the other four, so that they gave off smoke. The pile that represented Rhode Island was filled with brimstone, tar, and feathers, and the smell was terrible. When all thirteen fires were finally blazing, the young people danced around them on the green. Several Indians who were present stood up in amazement and concluded that this must be a very great council.

The biggest celebration was in Philadelphia, the city where the Declaration of Independence and the Constitution were born. At dawn, the bells of Christ Church and a cannon salute from the ship *Rising Sun* made certain that none of the people overslept on such an important day. Ten ships in the harbor hoisted pennants—one to represent each of the states that had ratified. On the green, 17,000 people watched the largest parade they had ever seen—5,000 people were in the parade! Huge floats represented ten ships and events of American history. Everyone who had a uniform, wore it. Every trade and profession marched with its

Independence Hall today—restored to the way
it looked in 1787

own banners. Six hundred of the marchers were shoemakers. Seventeen different clergymen marched, each repre-
senting a different religion.

"The Rabbi of the Jews, locked in the arms of two ministers," said Dr. Benjamin Rush. "It was a most delightful
sight."

Ten gentlemen, one from each of the states that had
adopted the Constitution, marched arm in arm to show
"union." As night came on, the ten ships in the harbor were
illuminated with hundreds of lanterns. No American had
ever seen such a spectacle. The high point of the day was
when James Wilson stood on a structure thirty-six feet high.
It was called "the Grand Federal Edifice" and was supposed
to represent the country. Unfortunately for James Wilson,

The Triumphal Arches at Gray's Ferry, ready
for George Washington's arrival

no one heard his speech that day. Thirteen cannons across
the river had chosen that moment to begin booming out
their part of the celebration.

Huzza the President

The next year it was New York's turn to put on the ex-
travaganzas, and New Yorkers did not wait until the last
minute to start. The year was 1789, and the new government that so many people had said could never succeed was
about to start. On Tuesday evening, March 3, the guns of the

New York Battery began firing at sunset. They began again at dawn on March 4, and all the bells in the city rang as the first congressmen took their seats.

Even in Boston the bells rang loudly for the congressmen from Massachusetts who were starting their new jobs in New York that day. Some boys, hearing the bells ring, cried "Fire!" A countryman's horse shied and took off with the turnip cart at his heels. He ran over a cellar door and the cart upset. A Boston man watching all this said, "This day is *really* the birthday of American Independence."

When the votes for President were counted on April 7,

The people of Trenton, New Jersey, greet Washington as the general who saved them from the enemy during the war

1789, there were 69 for George Washington John Adams had 34, so he became Vice President. The other men who received votes at that first election were John Jay–9; R. H. Harrison–6; John Hancock–4; John Rutledge–6; George Clinton–3; Samuel Huntington–2; John Milton–2; James Armstrong–1; Benjamin Lincoln–1; and Edward Telfair–1.

George Washington, the farmer, had a new job to do. He set out from his farm at Mount Vernon for New York. He was not at all sure he could do this job, but then there had been a day that he had not been sure he could lead an army fighting for independence either. Since he had little time to make the trip—the inaugural was to be on April 30, he traveled alone and Martha was to follow later.

Probably Washington needed those days and the long trip to encourage him for the job he was to do. From the day he set out from Mount Vernon, he began to realize how much people thought of him. Each town he went through sent out a "guard of honor." Sometimes their uniforms were made up of whatever finery the local people could find. But Washington, with his clothes completely covered by dust, did not look so fine either.

Every bridge was decorated with green boughs, arches of laurel, and colorful banners. Every few miles he was met by groups of people who wanted to give him greetings, or wreaths of laurel, or just shake hands. The people noticed his modesty immediately and heaved sighs of relief. No one, including George Washington, had any idea what a President should be like or how he should be addressed, but at least he had no royal airs about him.

When Washington reached Trenton, he passed under an arch of evergreens. On both sides were ladies and young girls in white robes, throwing flowers and covering him with

Washington takes the oath of office on April 30, 1789, on the balcony of Federal Hall in New York

wreaths. The song they sang reminded him of that wintry night when he had crossed the Delaware with his troops.

Welcome mighty chief once more
Welcome to this grateful shore
Now no mercenary foe
Aims again the hostile blow
Aims at thee the fatal blow.

From Elizabeth, New Jersey, Washington rode in a barge decorated with an awning and red curtains. Instead of sailing, the barge was rowed by twenty-six New York harbor pilots, thirteen on each side, who were dressed in white smocks and wore black-fringed hats. As the barge passed Staten Island, cannons fired and every ship hung every banner its crew could find. A Spanish warship, which had larger cannons than any American ship, very kindly added their booming to the celebration.

As the barge moved closer to Manhattan, a small sloop tacked close to the side and two men and two women began singing at the top of their lungs. The tune was "God Save the King," but the words were about the united states. Whether the words used were "My Country, 'Tis of Thee" is not recorded. Soon more sloops came close, their occupants singing loudly.

Washington landed in New York on April 23 with time to spare. The landing at the foot of Wall Street had been carpeted with crimson rug and even the railings were upholstered. After the new President was greeted by the governor of New York, Clinton, thousands of people cheered "Huzza, Huzza!" (Hooray! became the Americanized form of Huzza!) Then Washington did something that endeared him to the people forever. Instead of riding in the carriage to his house a half mile away, he walked.

At dawn on April 30, the cannons began booming again. It was the first Inauguration Day. Washington was to ride in a huge state coach—the kind once reserved for lords from England. He was dressed in a plain brown suit made of Connecticut cloth. Some people may have been slightly disappointed, but the lesson was unmistakable. Everything the new President wore had been made in America.

As he entered the Senate chamber, he bowed to the members of Congress. John Adams tried to speak and stumbled.

"Sir," said Adams finally, "the Senate and House of Representatives are ready to attend you to take the oath required by the Constitution."

"I am ready," said Washington.

They went out on the small balcony. Washington bowed to the people and sat down. A large Bible rested on a red pillow on a small table. After the oath, the group went back inside. When Washington stood to speak, the audience stood also. Neither they nor Washington seemed to know quite what was proper. After the speech, Washington went to a church service and went home to eat dinner alone.

Along the streets, the people watching their first President were pleased.

"Well, he deserves it all," said one.

"Now, I can die contented. I have seen George Washington," said another.

10

Birthing a New Country

> . . . busy in combatting the Convention . . . a nest
> of vipers disturbing the tranquility of govern-
> ment to answer selfish purposes.
> From Noah Webster's diary, March 27, 1784

Matters were not going at all well after the British soldiers
and Loyalists left American shores. The new American flag
was being insulted in different parts of the world. Mo-
hammedans held Americans hostage and made slaves of
them. An unruly mob, led by Daniel Shays, rioted in Massachusetts against the taxes they said were making poor people lose their homes.

The government owed money to everyone—from patriots who had loaned all their money to help win the war to
people like the widow Amy Dardin, who had been promised
payment for a horse taken during wartime and had never
received it. Every member of Congress came to know Amy
because she tried for the next thirty-two years to get her
money. Even the soldiers who had fought in the war had not
been paid. But the united states had no money.

"A republican government is almost the last kind of government I should choose now," said a disgruntled young man. "I'd sooner be subject to the caprice of one man than to the ignorance of a multitude."

Luckily, not many Americans agreed with him. There was a way to solve the country's problems. The thirteen American republics needed to be united under one strong government with a good Constitution. No one wanted the "nest of vipers" whom Noah Webster had dealt with only a few years before running the country.

In September of 1786, while Daniel Shays was still causing trouble in New England, a convention was held at Annapolis. It was a flop because nobody went. Before the next convention, in May of 1787, every local newspaper told people how very important it was for them to get together and vote for someone to represent them at the convention in Philadelphia.

The message went straight to the heart of Americans. Joseph Bachelor was just one who began attending meetings at parishes and districts. In February he wrote, "We had a Perrish meting to se if the Perrish wold rase monney to seport Govermend and to se if they wold chuse 1 man or more to send to Convenshan."

To Approve or Not

That summer, when the Constitutional Convention met, all the states were represented—except Rhode Island. By the end of summer, the Convention had decided on a Constitution and signed it on September 17. Now came the hard part. It must be approved by each of the thirteen states—or at least a majority of them. The entire Constitution was printed in every newspaper in the country so that every American could read it or have it read. But while the members of Congress waited for the approval, there were many other problems to solve, and they didn't waste time.

From each of the thirteen states came inventive ideas for running the country. A new idea was tried out carefully in one state. When people found that it worked, they adopted it for the whole country. New Jersey citizens put *e pluribus unum* on their coins. Americans liked that motto—one out of many—and soon it was put on all the copper coins. Another state tried out basing its money on the decimal system . . . one hundred pennies equaled one dollar. When people saw that the system worked well in one state, they chose it for the whole country. What looked like a multitude of people running a country turned into an advantage that still is unique to the united states.

The thirteen states were beginning to multiply. In addition to the independent state of Kentucky, the people who lived in the Green Mountains had formed the independent state of Vermont. Another large group of "downeasters" from northern Massachusetts were asking to become an independent state, too. So were the people who lived in the independent state of Franklin, but they never did succeed in having Congress approve their independence from North Carolina. All the newborn states had to wait until Congress met under the new Constitution to be voted into the union.

One problem that was solved without any waiting was the mails. Now that the war was over, the postriders no longer had to travel roundabout routes to avoid meeting British patrols. Until now, the only way a person could send a letter to a friend or relative was to find someone going to that person's city who would promise to deliver it. Starting in 1787, the mail was carried in stage carriages three times a week from May to November and twice a week during the winter months. Mail was not delivered to homes, but to "post offices" in taverns and general stores.

The government tried to solve the problem of paying the Revolutionary soldiers by giving them "bounty land." Unfortunately, an old soldier had to travel miles and spend years getting the papers together to prove he was deserving of the land. The government was also not very careful about whose land it gave away to the soldiers. Georgia soldiers were offered bounty land between the Oconee and Chattahoochee Rivers. When they went to claim it, they discovered the land was a Creek Indian hunting ground and included several Creek towns. Both groups claimed they had rights to the land and so there was trouble.

Worrisome Problems

The Indians were often pushed into signing peace treaties which they regretted doing at once and then did not know what to do about it. Wise old chiefs found themselves double-crossed by hot-blooded young braves who would have sold their grandmothers for whiskey. When the chiefs banished the troublemakers from their tribes, the outcasts formed gangs and committed atrocities for which the tribe was blamed. Luckily for Americans who lived near Indians and who were pushing west to settle in new country, the Indian tribes had not yet joined together to fight the common enemy that was taking away their land.

Many ordinary Americans still wondered whether a republican form of government was going to work. Every time the newspapers referred to the wife of a congressman as "Lady This" or "Lady That," the people shuddered. Even George Washington was not sure what to call himself. He turned down "Highness" quickly, but should he be an "Excellency"? The members of Congress did not know whether to refer to his inauguration speech as "his most gracious speech," as they would have said of a king, or just drop the "most gracious."

Some Americans even dropped in on Washington and other government heads to see whether their furniture was gold and velvet. One man reported that Alexander Hamilton was not aristocratic enough. Hamilton's office had a plain pine table for a desk, covered with a green cloth. His records and papers were spread out on planks held up by sawhorses. Instead of having his secretary dress in velvet and in silk stockings, Hamilton let the little man wear a long gray linen jacket and gray trousers. It was obvious that the Secretary of the Treasury was not taking any of the country's money for himself.

Lonely at the Top

George Washington was filled with worries of another sort. He was afraid that war was coming, perhaps with France. He wrote dozens of notes to generals and other advisers, asking all sorts of questions. Where would the French be likely to invade? What would happen if the French became possessors of Florida or Louisiana? How did the French usually form a line of battle? Did they use pikes? Should American soldiers be armed with pikes?

There were smaller matters too. His army had no uniforms. What sort of uniform would be good? What kind of badge should each man wear so anyone could tell a private from a general? Could he replace the black cockade that looked so British with something like a small eagle of pewter or silver? Would flannel be good for shirting and coat linings?

Washington was desperate for someone to advise him. One day, he decided to go to the Senate and ask for some advice. But he spent a day listening to the senators argue and debate, competing with the loud noise outside the chamber, until he could stand it no longer. He left, saying, "I'll be damned if I'll ever go there again!" And he didn't— nor has any President since Washington. It was then that a Cabinet was provided so the President could get some advice from men capable of giving it.

The entire army now numbered 840 men. Not even the promise of a "new suit" in 1788 had brought new recruits. The old system of getting a man drunk and then signing him up for the army had produced soldiers who deserted at critical moments. Now each recruit would get a bounty of $6, but not all at once and not until he showed up at training camp. To be a soldier, a man had to be 5 feet 6 inches tall without shoes, healthy, between the ages of 18 and 45, and white.

Then each man was to take the oath:

I do Solemnly Swear to bear true allegiance to the United States of America and to serve *them* honestly and faithfully against all *their* enemies or Opposers whomsoever and to Observe and to Obey the orders of the President of the United States of America and the orders of the Officers appointed over me according to the Articles of War.

Every man in the united states between 18 and 53 automatically belonged to his state militia. They met once a year, elected officers, drilled with sticks if they had no muskets, and then went home. Washington was afraid the country needed more of an army than that. There was one way to find out how many men could be called up in time of war and also to learn how many families were living in the country. An accurate count of citizens was needed, anyway, so that representatives for them could be chosen for Congress. The solution was to take a census—the first one ever in the new world.

Four Million Citizens

The census of 1790 showed that the united states now had 3,929,000 people. Many of the soldiers who had fought in the Revolution were now the heads of large families, teaching their children the joys of living in a free country, even though a great many of those people did not have freedom themselves.

Among the older men listed were many familiar names. Paul Revere was back in his silversmith shop, turning out bells and cannons. Patrick Henry was working hard as a lawyer, trying to save enough money to buy land so he could retire in a few years. John Hancock had become the governor of Massachusetts, and General Horatio Gates was living in New York state. George Rogers Clark was never paid for the money he spent during the war and now he was back surveying, with bitter feelings.

Many of the men listed were still to give much service to the new country. James Madison had run for the Senate, but ended in the House of Representatives. James Monroe had run for the House, but landed in the Senate. John Quincy Adams, a young and struggling lawyer, had only a few clients. A young man named Andrew Jackson had just gambled away all his inheritance on horse racing and now he was working hard as a lawyer in a state called Tennessee which he had helped to name.

Among the 757,208 black people listed was Benjamin Banneker, one of six men chosen to work with Pierre L'Enfant in laying out the new Federal City (later called "Washington City"). When L'Enfant had an argument with President Washington and went home to France, taking the plans for the city with him, it was Banneker whose photographic memory recalled the plan's important features. Banneker, an astronomer and mathematician, had just predicted an eclipse of the sun in 1789 and was about to publish an almanac. James Armistead, who had won the praise of Lafayette for spying during the war, had been freed and was now retired in New Kent County, Virginia. Seymour Burr, whose master was Aaron Burr's brother, had also been freed because of his war service and now lived in Massachusetts. But Samuel Charlton, who had gone to war at age sixteen in place of his master, had returned to slavery and was not freed until his master's death. An angry young black man named Richard Allen had left a Philadelphia church because he had been told to sit in the gallery "with other people of color." He was found by the 1790 census as the minister of his own newly formed Bethel Church.

Paul Cuffee, the son of a freedman, was thirty-one in 1790 and a prosperous shipowner devoted to bettering the lives of other black people. Prince Hall, a property owner in Boston, was trying to get public schools for black children in that city. James Forten, age twenty-four, had sailed on a privateer during the Revolution and was now apprenticed to a sailmaker. Before long, Forten would buy the business and become wealthy himself. James Derham, born a slave in Philadelphia, had been owned by several doctors and was now a qualified doctor himself at age twenty-eight.

On the Way to Fame

Among the youth, listed only as numbers in the census, were such people as Meriwether Lewis and William Clark, who would soon join the army. In Virginia, seventeen-year-old William Henry Harrison was on the way to the Presidency, but he didn't suspect it. In 1790, he had gone to medical school to please his father. When his father died the next year, Harrison would join the army. Michael Fink, at nineteen, was a keelboat man, born in Pittsburgh. He said he was "half horse, half alligator." At sixteen, John Chapman was just as crazy about farming as Mike was about boating. Neither youth could have dreamed that Mike Fink and Johnny Appleseed would become American legends.

The youngest people listed on the 1790 census would have to wait a while to leave their mark on the world. Stephen Decatur was to be a naval hero. Francis Scott Key would be inspired to write "The Star-spangled Banner." Zebulon Pike would be an explorer and have a Rocky Mountain peak named for him. Thomas Lincoln would have a famous son named Abraham. James Lawrence would head for the navy and be remembered for saying, "Don't give up the ship." But in 1790, all these little boys were between nine and thirteen years old. Among the very little children were Zachary Taylor, age 6; Winfield Scott, 4; Emma Hart (Willard), 3; Sarah Josepha Buell (Hale), 2; and David Crockett, 4, who had already shot his first bear.

Some of the people to play an important part in the new country were probably not listed in the census at all. Robert Fulton, whose steamboat *Clermont* was to pave the way for a new kind of transportation, was busily studying portrait painting in London. A French-Canadian miner digging lead ore on the bluffs of the Mississippi River gave his name to a city, but not the census: Julien Dubuque. Tecumseh was then a young Shawnee warrior, and Black Hawk a Sauk chief. A tiny Indian Shoshoni girl was about to be captured by another Indian tribe. She would be sold to a French-Canadian trader and, with him, would lead Lewis and Clark through the wild, uncharted country to the west. Her name was Sacagawea.

A Country to Reckon With

By the time the first census counted the American citizens, people were no longer worrying about raising enough food in their "uncivilized soil" to feed themselves. They had not turned the same color as the native Indians by living in a savage country, and their children's growth was not stunted. Even the hot summers and cold winters were not too uncomfortable when they designed their homes and clothing to cope with the changeable climate.

The country was no longer a collection of separate states. It was now a single United States, with a President, a capital city, a new Constitution, some newly added states, and a flag. That flag had just made its first voyage around the world, reminding every nation from China to Africa that a new country existed on the globe. Now, in 1790, Captain Robert Gray was sailing his American flagship back to the Pacific coast. When he discovered and sailed into the mouth of the Columbia River in 1792, he planted the new American flag on the land. In years to come, when the United States wanted to claim the Oregon Territory as its own, Captain Robert Gray's symbolic gesture helped to prove that claim of ownership. Perhaps Gray was a little optimistic that day in 1792, but that is the way we, the people, were in the years 1783 to 1793.

11

FINDING 1787 TODAY

"It would be fun to go back to those days—
just for a little while."

You can do it. Take a picnic lunch or eat in an eighteenth-
century tavern. Wander through a re-created village and
shut out the modern world for a few hours. You will find
hundreds of houses standing just where they were two cen-
turies ago—like the Paul Revere house in Boston, or the
house where Noah Webster (you met him as a young lover
in this book) was born in West Hartford, Connecticut. Or
you may drive off the Interstate Highway into a small town
that used to be an important city two hundred years ago and
find that it still has many 1787 houses and some of that
peaceful, old-fashioned flavor, like Edenton, North Carolina,
or New Castle in Delaware.

But if you want to spend a whole afternoon sampling life
in the 1780s, here are some places worth detouring off the
turnpikes to see. Some cost only a little more than a movie
to visit, but many of them are free. Have a good trip back
into history.

181

What Is There to See and Do?

New Hampshire

Portsmouth

STRAWBERY BANKE: Has 30 buildings dating from 1695 to 1820. A weaver, blacksmith, potter, leatherworker, and silversmith can be seen at work. Open daily 9:30–5 May 1–Oct. 31.

Vermont

Shelburne

SHELBURNE MUSEUM: An outdoor museum with 35 buildings of both the 18th and the 19th century. Includes sidewheeler steamer, railroad, stagecoach inn, general store. Folk art, dolls, quilts, coaches. Open daily 9–5 mid-May to mid-Oct.

Massachusetts

Deerfield

HISTORIC DEERFIELD: This was a thriving town in 1787, and a dozen homes standing then are still there today. Open 9:30–4:30 Mon.–Sat.; 1–4:30 Sun.

Salem

ESSEX INSTITUTE: Houses and a museum covering other periods as well as 1787. Open daily, but closed Mondays from Oct. 15 through Dec.

SALEM MARITIME NATIONAL HISTORIC SITE: Has old custom-house, wharf and merchant's house from 1787, and West India Goods Store. Open daily.

Saugus

SAUGUS IRON WORKS NATIONAL HISTORIC SITE: A good place to see how iron was made. Ironworks house built 1648. See the blast furnace, forge, blacksmith shop. Open daily 9–5 April through Oct.; 9–4 Nov. through March.

Sturbridge

OLD STURBRIDGE VILLAGE: This re-created farming village takes you from 1790 to 1840. Forty original buildings were moved to this 200-acre site. Homes, shops, craftsmen. Open daily 9:30–5:30 April through Nov. Open 10–4 Tues. through Sun. from Dec. through March.

Connecticut

Danbury

SCOTT-FANTON MUSEUM: Has a 1784 house, a 1790 hat shop, textile and craft exhibits. Open 2–5 Wed.–Sun.; closed holidays.

Mystic

MYSTIC SEAPORT MUSEUM: You can lose yourself in this historic seaport. Even though its date is about 1850, much of the 1790 seaport life is shown here. Open daily 9–5 April through Nov. Open 10–4 Dec. through March.

Simsbury

SIMSBURY HISTORIC CENTER: Costumes, an 18th-century house with ballroom, schoolhouse, carriage house. Open daily 1–4 May 1 through Oct. Some buildings open Nov. through April.

Rhode Island

Pawtucket

SLATER MILL HISTORIC SITE: Here is the mill begun in 1789 and the old 1793 mill building still standing. Open 10–5 Tues.–Sat. and 1–5 Sun. from June 1 to Sept. 5.

New York

Cooperstown

FARMER'S MUSEUM: This museum, in a town begun in 1786, has

demonstrations and equipment of early American farming, wool and flax spinning. Country store, school, blacksmith shop, tavern, church, printshop, apothecary. Open daily 9–5 May through Oct.; the rest of the year 9–5 Tues.–Sat.; 1–5 Sun.

Mumford (near Rochester)

GENESEE COUNTRY VILLAGE: If you want to see life just after 1793 and into the early 1800s, this village has 50 buildings moved from nearby areas and restored. Villagers in costume show how the early inhabitants baked, cooked, spun and wove cloth, made pottery and tins. Also a Gallery of Sporting Art. Open daily 10–5 mid-May to mid-Oct.

Pennsylvania

Bedford

OLD BEDFORD VILLAGE: Has 30 buildings from frontier 1750 to 1850. Log cabins and schools brought from their original sites. Crafts include gunmaking, quilting, tinsmithing, shoemaking. Open daily 9–5 mid-April to mid-Oct.

Bethlehem

18TH CENTURY INDUSTRIAL AREA: Restored tannery, springhouse, waterworks, all operating in 1787. Many other crafts and trades. Open 10–4 Tues.–Sat.

Near Birdsboro (Morgantown exit on Pa. Turnpike)

HOPEWELL VILLAGE: Remains of an ironmaking village built about 1740, which supplied cannons for the Revolution in addition to cast-iron stoves, hollow ware, kettles. Many buildings. National Historic Site. Open daily 9–5.

Cornwall

CORNWALL IRON FURNACE: You can visit a furnace that produced stoves, tools, cannons, cannonballs even before 1787 and long after. Open 9–5 Wed–Sat. late April to late Oct. Shorter hours 10–4:30 the rest of the year.

Edgemont

COLONIAL PENNSYLVANIA PLANTATION: A real pioneer farm with demonstrations. In Ridley Creek State Park. Open daily in summer.

Ephrata

EPHRATA CLOISTER: An 18th-century communal society, famous for its music and printing. Has 10 original buildings. Includes a musical drama of 18th-century life in summer. Open 9–5 Tues.–Sat.; 12–5 Sun. late April to late Oct. Open 10–4:30 the rest of the year, but closed on many holidays.

Philadelphia

PHILADELPHIA: The people who lived two hundred years ago could find many familiar landmarks today, most of them centered in the Independence National Park. Look for the 1787 State House (now called Independence Hall), Liberty Bell, Carpenters' Hall, City Tavern, Benjamin Franklin Court, Betsy Ross House, Congress Hall, Kosciuszko House, Bishop White House, Head House Square, Dolley Payne Todd House, Pemberton House. Most open daily.

Near Towanda

AZILUM: In 1793, French patriots began building this log city as a refuge for nobles who managed to escape from the French Revolution. It is now being restored. Five log cabins finished. Open 9–5 Wed.–Sat. during Daylight Saving Time; 10–4:30 the rest of the year. 10–4:30 Sun. Closed holidays.

New Jersey

Batsto

BATSTO IRON WORKS: This is a good place to see life and industry in a village famous in 1787 for its iron furnace. See the furnace site, mansion, sawmill, gristmill. Open daily 10–6 May 30 to Labor Day; 11–5 the rest of the year.

Clinton

CLINTON HISTORICAL MUSEUM VILLAGE: The flaxseed mill here was going strong in 1787. See also the blacksmith shop, general store, log cabin, school, pottery shop. Open 1–4 Mon.–Fri.; weekends 12–5 from April 1 to Oct. 31. Closed holidays.

Stanhope

WATERLOO VILLAGE: Restored early American buildings in a village over 30 years old in 1787. Has an inn, church, blacksmith shop, gristmill, carriage house. Open 10–6 Tues.–Sun. and holidays mid-April through Dec.

Delaware

New Castle

NEW CASTLE: This is one of the few towns today in which 18th-century persons could find their way around. The Green and many of the homes, churches, and buildings were old in 1787. Most open daily.

Maryland

Annapolis

ANNAPOLIS: Another city that has not lost its 1780s look. It has the same waterfront and many of its original buildings. From the dock, you can take a boat ride across Chesapeake Bay to St. Michael's, Maryland, another old village famous as a shipbuilding port in 1787. Or take a boat trip to Oxford, Maryland, a famous port in 1787.

Towson

HAMPTON NATIONAL HISTORIC SITE: This is the grandest home in the new united states, begun in 1783. Open 11–4:30 Tues.–Sat.; 1–5 Sun.

Virginia

Alexandria

OLD TOWN ALEXANDRIA: This is the same old town that 1787 people found so elegant. An 18-block walking tour includes shops, taverns, homes—all standing right there two hundred years ago. Stop at Ramsay House for information. Open daily 10–5.

Charlottesville

MICHIE TAVERN MUSEUM: Not far from Monticello was a tavern where Jefferson was often a guest. Has an interesting kitchen with some "modern" inventions, ballroom, keeping-hall, ladies parlor bedroom, bar, log cabin built by Jefferson, and an "ordinary" that serves colonial food (a slave house in 1787). Open daily 9–5.

MONTICELLO: Thomas Jefferson began building his home in 1769, had been living here long before 1787, and is buried here. You will find many of Jefferson's own inventions and a good idea of a Virginia gentleman's life. Open daily 8–5 from Mar. 1 to Oct. 31. Open 9–4:30 the rest of the year.

Fredericksburg

HISTORIC FREDERICKSBURG: Here is another city that puts you into the 18th century. See where James Monroe was practicing law from 1786 to 1791; Hugh Mercer's Apothecary Shop; the homes of George Washington's sister and mother; the home he lived in as a boy, and the tavern built by his brother. Most are open daily.

Mount Vernon

MOUNT VERNON: This is the country home which Washington left reluctantly to become the first President in 1789 and the place where he and Martha are buried. The home contains many of the original furnishings, restored greenhouse quarters, stables, kitchen, gardens. Open daily 9–5 March through Oct.; open 9–4 the rest of the year.

Williamsburg

COLONIAL WILLIAMSBURG: Noah Webster said this city was dying in 1787, because it was no longer the capital of Virginia. No less than 88 buildings show you life there during the 18th century and into the early 1800s. You can see every early craft, people in costume, and you can often have a candlelight evening tour as well. Buildings open daily 9–5 and on some summer evenings.

Throughout Virginia

PLANTATIONS: If you want to sample 18th-century plantation life, Virginia has many plantations. For example, Haw Branch (at Amelia); Smithfield (Blacksburg); Red Hill, which was Patrick Henry's (at Brookneal); Brandon, designed by Thomas Jefferson (at Burrowsville); Berkeley and Shirley Plantations (at Charles City); Castle Hill (at Cismont); Stratford Hall (at Stratford); and Chippokes (at Surry).

North Carolina

Cherokee

CHEROKEE INDIAN MUSEUM: If you are interested in Indian history, this museum, as well as the Cyclorama of the Cherokee Indian and the Oconaluftee Indian Village show how the Indians lived. Museum open 9–5:30; evenings in summer, Mon.–Sat. Cyclorama open 9–9 summer; 9–6 the rest of the year. Indian Village open 9–5:30 mid-May through Oct.

Halifax

HISTORIC HALIFAX: This state historical site has a restored colonial village. It was an important river port in 1787. Open 9–5 Tues.–Sat.; 1–5 Sun.

Near Wilmington on Cape Fear River

BRUNSWICK TOWN: A ghost of a colonial village. You won't see fine homes here, but you will see excavated foundations and archaeological exhibits of a town that had disappeared by 1787 and has been found again. State Historic Site. Open 9–5 Tues.–Sat.; 1:30–5 Sun.

Near Winston-Salem

HISTORIC BETHABARA PARK: A thriving eighteenth-century trade and crafts center. Now you can visit the church, potter's house, reconstructed fort, museum. Open 9:30–4:30 Mon.–Fri.; 1:30–4:30 weekends.

OLD SALEM VILLAGE: Has 54 restored buildings dating from 1766 to mid-19th century. Be sure to see the tavern, single brothers' house, boys' school. Open 9:30–4:30 Mon.–Sat.; 1:30–4:30 Sun.

South Carolina

Charleston

CHARLESTON: The early "Charles Town" of 1787 is still here with many old homes, the oldest synagogue in continuous use, old powder magazine, slave mart, seaport, museum with apothecary shop, first theater, and outside the city are some of the gardens and plantations that were famous.

Throughout South Carolina

SOUTH CAROLINA PLANTATIONS: Plantation life around 1787 can still be found at places like Boone Hall and Middleton Place (near Charleston), Hopsewee (Georgetown), and Walnut Grove (near Spartanburg), Magnolia Plantation and Gardens (Charleston).

Georgia

Savannah

SAVANNAH: This was a small town in 1787, not yet as important as Sunbury, Georgia, which no longer exists. After Sherman's "March through Georgia," few homes of the 18th century were left standing. One of the few places his men missed is Midway, a small town near Savannah. Here is a handsome church built in 1792 and an 18th-century building next door with a museum. Open 9–5 Tues.–Sat.; 2–5:30 Sun.

Picture Credits

The author and the readers of this book are indebted to the following generous people and groups for the chance to see America as it looked to its first citizens by permitting the use of rarely seen drawings, many of them published in 1783–1793 magazines:

Mr. Whitfield Bell and the American Philosophical Society, for the pictures on pages 20, 21, 53, 66, 80, 91, 94, 101, 114, 115, 124, 127, 164, 165.

Eno Collection; Art, Prints and Photographs Division of The New York Public Library; Astor, Lenox and Tilden Foundations, for the picture on pages 118, 167.

The National Park Service of the U.S. Department of the Interior, for photographs on pages 17, 23, 29, 85, 102, 121, 154, 161, 163.

The Insurance Company of North America Museum for the pictures on pages 139, 141.

The Library of Congress for the picture on page 31; and for the picture on page 34 from Harper's New Monthly Magazine of November, 1854.

The Free Library of Philadelphia's Rare Book Room for the pictures on pages 39, 42, 47, 56, 61, 63, 144.

BIBLIOGRAPHY

Here are some of the books and magazines I read to find out about life two hundred years ago:

American Heritage magazines from 1969 on.

Cosmopolitan Magazine, "A Society Girl of the 18th Century," March 1901.

A Dictionary of Americanisms on Historical Principles, ed. by Mitford McLeod Mathews. University of Chicago Press, 1951.

Earle, Alice Morse, *Home Life in Colonial Days: Written in the Year 1898.* Berkshire Traveller Press, 1974.

George Washington: A Biography in His Own Words, ed. by Ralph K. Andrist. Published by Newsweek, distributed by Harper & Row, 1972.

Kiefer, Monica, *American Children Through Their Books 1700–1835.* University of Pennsylvania Press, 1948.

Langdon, William Chauncy, *Everyday Things in American Life,* Vol. 2: 1776–1876. Charles Scribner's Sons, 1941.

Lantz, Louise K., *Old American Kitchenware 1725–1925.* Thomas Nelson & Sons, 1970.

McIlvaine, Paul, *The Dead Town of Sunbury, Ga.* Paul McIlvaine, Publisher, 1971.

Ramsay, David, *Memoirs of the Life of Martha Laurens Ramsay.* 3d ed. Boston, printed and sold by Samuel Etheridge, Charleston, 1812.

Ravenel, Harriet Horry, *Women of Colonial and Revolutionary Times.* South Carolina Heritage Series, No. 10. The Reprint Co., 1967.

Sellers, Charles Coleman, *Mr. Peale's Museum.* W. W. Norton & Co., 1980.

Sheftall, John McKay, *Sunbury on the Medway.* State of Georgia, 1977.

Slave Testimony, ed. by John W. Blassingame. Louisiana State University Press, 1977.

Spruill, Julia Cherry, *Women's Life and Work in the Southern Colonies.* University of North Carolina Press, 1938.

The Story of America as Reported by Its Newspapers, 1690–1965, ed. by Edwin Emery. Simon & Schuster, 1965.

This Was America, ed. by Oscar Handlin. Harvard University Press, 1949; reissued 1969.

Next, to find out more about people two hundred years ago, I read the books, magazines, and newspapers that they were reading. Here are the books:

Accurate Description of North America, by a man from Rotterdam who lived over twenty years with the Indians. 1780.

Amusement Hall: Introduction to Useful Knowledge. Philadelphia, 1796.

The Art of Speaking. 6th ed. New York, 1786.

Benezet, *The Pennsylvania Spelling Book or Youth's Friendly Instructor and Monitor.* Providence, R. I., 1783 (?).

Berquin, *The Children's Friend.* London, 1783.

Brissot, Jean Pierre, *Voyage dan les États-Unis de l'Amérique.* 1791.

Carter, Susannah, *The Frugal Housewife.* Philadelphia, 1796.

Crevecoeur, Hector St. J. de, *Letters from an American Farmer.* 1782.

Dilworth, Thomas, *The Schoolmaster's Assistant.* Philadelphia, 1784.

Farley, John, *The London Art of Cookery.* London, 1785.

Fisher, George, *The American Instructor or Young Man's Best Companion.* Philadelphia, 1787.

Franklin, Benjamin, *Information to those who would remove to America.* London, 1794.

Goldsmith, Oliver, *An History of the Earth and Animated Nature.* Philadelphia, 1795.

Greenwood, James, *The Philadelphia Vocabulary.* 1787.

Janeway, James, *A Token for Children.* 1781.

Kilner, M. A. M., *The Adventures of a Pincushion.* 1788.

A Little Pretty Pocket Book. Printed by Isaiah Thomas, Worcester, Mass., 1787.

Morse, Jedidiah, *Geography Made Easy.* New Haven, 1784.

The New England Primer, enlarged and much improved. Philadelphia, 1783.

One Thousand Valuable Secrets in the Elegant and Useful Arts. 1st American edition, printed for B. Davies, Philadelphia, 1795.

Osborne, Henry, *An English Grammar* adapted to the capacities of children. Charleston, 1785.

Ozanam, *Recreation for Gentlemen and Ladies.* Dublin, 1790.

Peddle, Mrs., *Rudiments of Taste,* letters from mothers to daughters. Philadelphia, 1789.

The History of Little Goody Two shoes; otherwise called Mrs. Margery Twoshoes. Printed by Isaiah Thomas, Worcester, Mass. 1787.

Rush, Benjamin, *Thoughts upon the Amusements and Punishments which are proper for school.* Pamphlet. 1790.

The School of Good Manners. Hartford, 1787.

Smith, E., *The Compleat Housewife or Accomplished Gentlewoman's Companion.* New York, 1765.

Solomon, S., M. D., *A Guide to Health.* Printed by author by J. Clarke, New York, 1800.

The Sportsman's Companion, or an Essay on Shooting, by a gentleman. 3d ed. Philadelphia, 1792.

These were the newspapers read by people who lived two hundred years ago:

Boston Centinel, 1788 on.

Charleston Morning Post and Daily Advertiser, 1786 on.

City Gazette and Daily Advertiser, Charleston, 1787–1788.

Columbian Herald and the General Advertiser, Charleston, 1793.

Columbian Herald or Independent Courier of North America, Charleston, 1787.

Independent Journal or the General Advertiser, New York, 1787 on.

Pennsylvania Evening Herald & American Monitor, 1785.

Pennsylvania Evening Post & Daily Advertiser, 1783.

Pennsylvania Packet & Daily Advertiser, Philadelphia, 1787 on.

Pittsburgh Gazette, Pittsburgh, 1786 on.

Royal Danish American Gazette, St. Thomas, V. I., 1787.

State Gazette of South Carolina, 1787 on.

In addition to newspapers, people between 1785 and 1790 were reading several magazines. Here are some that I read and borrowed pictures from:

The American Magazine, New York, 1787–88.

The American Museum, or Universal Magazine, 1787–89.

The American Musical Magazine, New Haven, 1786–87.

The Children's Magazine, Hartford, 1789.

Columbian Magazine or Monthly Miscellany, Philadelphia, 1786.

Gentlemen and Ladies' Town and Country Magazine, Boston, 1789–90.

Gentleman and Lady's Town and Country Magazine, Boston, 1784.

Ladies Magazine and Repository, Philadelphia, 1792.

Massachusetts Magazine or Monthly Museum of Knowledge and Rational Entertainment, 1789.

New Hampshire Magazine and Monthly Repository of Useful Information, Concord, 1793.

New Haven Gazette & The Connecticut Magazine, New Haven, 1786.

New Jersey Magazine and Monthly Advertiser, New Brunswick, 1786–87.

New York Magazine or Literary Depository, New York, 1790.

Universal Asylum and Columbian Magazine, Philadelphia, 1790.

The Worcester Magazine, Worcester, Mass., 1786.

No one could write about life almost two hundred years ago without hearing from the people who lived then—their hopes, dreams, thoughts, experiences. Here are some of the people who talked through their journals, diaries, and letters:

Frances Parke Custis, *cookbook,* from her daughter-in-law, Martha Washington
Sally Emerson, *prescription book,* 1795
Henry Wismer, *account book,* 1768 to 1800

Journals and Letters

Robert Ayres	Daniel Mulford
Joseph Bachelor	Mary Plumsted
Dr. Benjamin Smith Barton	General Rufus Putnam
Lewis Beebe	William Rollinson
Elizabeth Cranch	Catherine Saunders
Ebenezer Denny	Samuel Shepard
Elizabeth Drinker	Rebecca Shoemaker
Timothy Ford	Nathaniel R. Snowden
Holbrook Gaskill	Thomas Walcutt
James Gibson	George Washington
Norris Jones	Nathan Webb
Collin McGregor	Noah Webster

and many others whose names are unknown

For sights of 1783–1793 that can still be seen today, I used the American Automobile Association TourBooks, which are available to AAA members.

INDEX

Picture references are in italics

About the Author

SUZANNE HILTON was born in Pittsburgh, Pennsylvania, but a family pattern of moving often into strange new neighborhoods started an inquisitiveness that has never been curbed. She attended nearly a dozen schools from California to Pennsylvania before attending Pennsylvania College for Women (now Chatham College) in Pittsburgh and graduating from Beaver College in Glenside, Pennsylvania.

During World War II, she used her knowledge of languages as a volunteer in the Foreign Inquiry Department of the American Red Cross. After the war, she married Warren M. Hilton, an industrial and insurance engineer and Lt. Colonel, U.S. Army Reserve. With their son, Bruce, and daughter, Diana, the Hiltons traveled thousands of miles camping and sailing.

A busy free-lance writer, Suzanne Hilton has written ten books, nine of which have been Junior Literary Guild selections. She now lives in Jenkintown, Pennsylvania.